MY HEART TO GIVE

A MAXWELL FAMILY SAGA - BOOK THREE

S.B. ALEXANDER

RAVEN WING PUBLISHING

My Heart to Give
A Maxwell Family Saga - Book Three
Copyright © 2019 by S.B. Alexander
All rights reserved.
First Edition:
E-book ISBN-13: 978-1-7329767-4-0
Print ISBN-13: 978-1-7329767-5-7

Visit: http://sbalexander.com
Editor: Red Adept Editing
Cover Design by Hang Le

Chapter 1

Maiken

The cafeteria hummed with voices big and small. Utensils clanged together, and trays slapped on the tables as kids set down their food. Kensington High hadn't changed much since I'd walked out the doors back in June. What had changed? Or I should ask who had changed? Me. My family. My life.

Chaos and tension described how we were living. The twins, Emma and Ethan, my brother Marcus, and I had moved in with my cousin Kade and his wife, Lacey. Their brand-new home was modern, massive, and had more amenities than I'd ever seen. But *where* we lived wasn't in turmoil.

Marcus, a freshman in high school, was out of control. It seemed like he'd been in the principal's office every day for mouthing off to teachers or fighting. I shouldn't care so much. After all, he was a teenager, trying to find his way, trying to fit in. But I did care. I didn't want to see him hurt. I didn't want him to start off his first year in high school with a suspension. After all, I was his big brother, the oldest of eight children. So it was my duty to watch over him. But two weeks into the school year, trying to keep Marcus in line was proving to be a challenge.

Marcus reached over the table and snatched Ethan's hamburger.

Ethan went to slap his hand but missed. "You're a pig, man."

Flicking his shaggy light-brown hair from his forehead, Marcus shrugged. "I don't see you eating it."

My skin crawled with fury. "Stop being a dick, man." I didn't know how to get through to him, and neither did Kade, for that matter.

"Call me a dick one more time, and I'll throw the tray at you." His jaw was locked tight, and his blue eyes were swimming with a dare.

Even though he was fifteen years old, he almost matched Ethan and me in height. I was the tallest out of the three of us at six foot three. I'd grown another inch over the summer. I suspected all of us kids would be tall, considering my dad was six foot two and my mom wasn't a short lady either. Regardless, Marcus had grown to nearly six feet in the last several months, but that didn't mean he could win a fight with me.

I kicked the chair back and slapped two hands on the table. The exploding sound quieted the voices from nearby tables. "Try it."

Ethan swung out his arm and pushed me back down in my chair. "Not here."

My gut burned. I loved Marcus, but at the moment, rage was all I had for him.

"Yeah, I didn't think you had the balls to hit me," Marcus taunted.

Ethan narrowed his brown gaze. "Shut the fuck up. You might be brave enough to take on one of us, but you won't win if we both gang up on you." His tone brokered no argument. He sounded like our dad when he'd reprimanded one of us.

My gaze drifted past Marcus to the table of nosy kids gawking. "Mind your own business," I snapped like a dry twig. If anyone dared to take a picture, I would for sure smash the phone then maybe their hands.

Calm down, dude. You're acting like Marcus now.

I gave myself a mental shake, sucked in a quiet breath, then released the air in my lungs.

Ethan dragged bruised knuckles through his thick brown hair, which had grown out over the summer. "So, dude," he said to Marcus, "how does it feel to be in high school?"

I knew Ethan was trying to deflect or break the tension, but I wasn't sure school was the right topic to bring up.

Marcus's eyes became slits, and he chewed as though he hadn't eaten in a week. "Sucks if you ask me, especially with you two on my ass."

I kicked Marcus under the table.

He growled. "Is that all you got?"

Grinding my back teeth, I fisted my hands in my lap. He definitely needed an attitude adjustment. School wasn't the place to give him one, though.

I diverted my gaze from my brother to try to get my anger under control. Yet nothing would help unless Quinn walked into the cafeteria, and her lunch period didn't begin for another five minutes. Nevertheless, I spotted Dustin Lane at a table diagonal from us. I didn't know him that well, but I knew he was a big deal for the high school hockey team. I also knew he was dating Tessa Stevens again. Apparently, they'd been an item freshman year, had broken up, and now were reunited, which was great for me. That meant Tessa wasn't gunning to get her grabby hands all over me like she had been when I'd first enrolled at Kensington almost a year ago.

"Marcus, didn't you say you're into hockey?" I asked in an even tone.

Marcus loved boxing and rugby. Since we'd moved to Ashford, he'd gotten the hockey bug. "Why don't you try out for the hockey team this year?" Hockey was a physical sport. Checking and plowing into his opponents would help him release some of the aggression he had bottled up.

Basketball wasn't a contact sport like hockey, but just being out on the court took my mind away from my troubles. Quinn was also a shining star that always made me smile. Maybe Marcus needed a Quinn in his life too. But I couldn't force him to find a girlfriend. I couldn't force him to do much, come to think of it.

"That's a great idea," Ethan said. "Tryouts are coming up, I think."

Our dad had loved sports, any sport. He'd felt that being on a team built character. The military did as well, but that wasn't an option yet.

Marcus studied Ethan and me, thinking as he chewed.

Man, it would be great if he did take up hockey instead of causing trouble and mayhem. All of us were struggling with our dad's death, even a year later. We were also praying every day for our aunt Denise, who was battling stage IV breast cancer. She had her good days and bad according to Mom. But the future didn't look so good for my aunt.

"Well?" I asked.

He shoved the tray of food at me. "Stop trying to be Dad." Then he stalked off, swallowed up by the incoming crowd.

A low rumble rattled my chest while rage ate at the lining of my stomach like a starving animal. Yep, my junior year was off to a great start.

I'd promised my mom I would take care of Marcus, but that was going to be a huge feat. Kade was having trouble with him, too, which kind of surprised me because Kade was a big, scary dude when he was angry, and I'd seen him furious with Marcus more times than I cared to lately.

"Mom did the right thing in letting us live with Kade," Ethan said.

I harrumphed. "I don't know about that." But I would rather Kade and I deal with Marcus than my mom. She had her hands full with her sister and my four other siblings who were living with her in Georgia.

"Kade will get through to him," Ethan said. "I think he's still feeling Marcus out."

I cracked my knuckles. "Um… we've been living with Kade and Lacey since January. He's had nine months." In all fairness to Kade, Marcus had taken his rebellion up several notches when he'd started school.

"Maybe we should have one of those interventions," Ethan said. "You know, get him in a room with all of us and lay down the law."

I quirked an eyebrow. "Cornering a person never works. You should know that with the bruises on your hand."

"Hey, I was defending Marcus from the two dudes that were about to beat his face in."

Apparently, Marcus had pissed off some guy in his math class last week, and after school, the guy and his buddy had cornered Marcus in the parking lot. Luckily, Ethan had been walking up. Otherwise, I didn't want to think what could've happened.

I sighed. "It's going to be a long one if we can't get through to Marcus. We'll have to watch him like a hawk."

"I'll do my best, but I don't see freshmen much during the day."

He had a point. The school had separate wings for the freshmen, sophomores, juniors, and seniors, which made it hard to find my siblings during the day. The only time I did see them was during lunch, except for Emma. Her schedule was different because she was on the advanced placement track.

"Just keep your radar up," I said. "You know how kids talk. You'll hear about a fight before you see it anyway."

Ethan sighed. "Whatever."

I didn't like babysitting Marcus any more than he did. But family took care of their own—words my dad had always said—and I was finding that Kade and his dad had the same motto.

But mottos, brothers, and family slipped away when I spotted my girl sashaying toward me with a smile that was reserved only for me. Yeah, Quinn Thompson was my everything. No matter how bad things were in my life, she had a way of making me forget for the moment, making my stomach flutter, and making me believe that anything was possible.

She slid into the chair Marcus had vacated.

I frowned. "There's an empty chair here." I patted the one on the other side of me.

She rolled her gorgeous amber eyes, which were framed by long, thick lashes. "I can't stay long, and if I sit there, then you'll have your hands all over me."

So true. Lately, our relationship was climbing to the next level, as in touchy-feely territory. Kissing her was like walking on air, but exploring more of Quinn's body above the waist topped everything.

Memories flashed in my mind of Quinn in a bathing suit—a bikini to be exact. We'd spent most of August on the lake, and the first time she'd waltzed out in a bikini top, my jaw had dropped. My girl had breasts that I was sure other girls envied—round, big, and all mine. Sure, I'd known she had nice breasts when I met her, but seeing her in a bikini top was... Well, all I could say was *wow*!

Ethan pushed to his feet. "I'm out of here. You two make me want to vomit."

"You're just jealous you don't have a girl," I teased.

"It's better if I don't. You know that."

My brother was afraid to commit to anything, really. He was afraid we would move again. I couldn't blame him. I feared that could happen at any time if my mom decided that she wanted all of us with her in Georgia.

"I feel bad for Ethan," Quinn said.

Sliding down in my seat, I extended my leg under the table and ran my foot up her leg, grinning like an ass. "Don't. It's his decision."

Her head darted around the room. "What are you doing?" The shy Quinn I loved was blushing and worried about people seeing us.

"You don't want to sit next to me. So I have to find other ways to touch my girl."

She popped up so fast, I barely had time to track her moves before she was in Ethan's chair. "Listen, you big hunk." She giggled, turning to face me. "I thought you didn't like public displays of affection. Remember that night at Shaker's when you wouldn't kiss me?"

"Maybe I've grown." I leaned in until my lips and hers were a thread apart. "Big hunk, huh? Where did that come from?"

She squeezed my biceps. "Your muscles are bigger since you've been working out."

The entire basketball team had been on a workout and conditioning schedule since the season ended last year.

And your breasts are a little bigger. "You like?"

As seriously as she could, she said, "Nah. They're okay."

I pulled her chair closer to me then grabbed her waist. "I think you should rethink your answer." I was ready to tickle her, and man, she was ticklish.

She pursed her lips, holding in a laugh, and shook her head.

Wrong answer. I pressed my fingers into her waist.

She squealed, a sound I was finding I really, really liked coming out of her heart-shaped lips. But as much as I loved teasing her, I had to let go. The way my body was reacting wasn't appropriate for the cafeteria or any public place.

Regardless, it was becoming harder and harder not to do more than kiss her. I had ideas that my dad would probably counsel me not to act on until I was eighteen or maybe even married.

I playfully bit her lip. "Baby doll, try again."

Her eyes lit up. "Baby doll? That's a new one."

I'd heard Kade call Lacey that, and Lacey had melted. Not that Quinn didn't melt around me when I called her babe, but right then, I was digging how she was ten shades of red and fidgeting in her seat.

"So what's up?" I asked. A subject change was needed because my jeans were becoming extremely tight.

"I can't come over after school. My mom and I are taking Apple and Oscar out."

"Your mom? Since when does she ride horses?"

"She always has, silly. I guess I never told you. Do you want to come with? You can ride one of the other horses."

I snorted. "That's a no. I might be okay to brush them or feed them, but riding? No way."

She giggled. "I didn't think so. But I'll keep asking until you do. It would be fun to ride together. We could take the horses down into the woods behind the lake." She waggled her eyebrows.

Enticing as being alone with her in the woods sounded, I wasn't ready to get on a horse. I'd had an aversion to them since I was a kid.

But horses and Quinn went by the wayside when a petite girl with wide brown eyes and short white-blond hair dropped into a chair across the table from Quinn and me. "Which one of you is Maiken Maxwell?"

I heard the question but was riveted on how the girl's red lace bra poked out of her low-cut T-shirt.

Idiot. Take your eyes off her. Your girl is next to you.

"Do I look like a Maiken to you?" Quinn asked.

When the girl shrugged, her cleavage became more pronounced. I didn't ogle other girls, but it was hard to look away. Her boobs were practically on the table as she leaned forward.

"Quinn could be a boy's name. Maiken could be a girl's name," Nose Piercing Girl said easily as the glare from the sun sprayed in through the large windows.

I guess she had a point. "I'm Maiken."

The girl sized me up as far as she could see me. "Mm. Maiken, huh? Cool name. Where did you get it?"

"The local Walmart," I replied, using the same snarky attitude as her.

She bobbed her head. "Good one."

Quinn jutted out her chin. "Who are you?"

"New girl. You got a beef with that?" she asked.

"What do you want with me?" I asked.

Her barely there eyebrows lifted. "I could think of a few things."

Quinn snapped her fingers at the girl. "He's my boyfriend. So don't get any ideas."

New Girl sat back, picking at a nail. "Testy." Then as though she didn't care about Quinn or anyone else, she smiled at me. "You're my tutor in physics."

Quinn's gaze rounded on me. "Since when?"

That was news to me. All I could do was shrug.

Chapter 2
Quinn

A chill in the air made me shiver as I ran into school. I had fifteen minutes to get to my locker, get my math notebook, which I'd forgotten the day before, rush into class, and do my homework.

I opened my locker, looking around for Maiken. I was hoping to catch him before first period. I hadn't had a chance to talk to him the night before. After horseback riding, Momma and I had spent the rest of the evening stocking shelves in the farm store with new products.

I was curious if he'd found out any more about being a tutor. He'd seemed as shocked as I'd been when the new girl had given him the news. Not that he couldn't tutor anyone, but Maiken's free time was consumed with basketball and getting ready for the season. Which led me to believe the new girl had been pulling his chain. It was clear that she wanted his attention. She'd all but flopped her breasts onto the table, showing off her cleavage and her bra, which had been on display.

I had thought junior year would be smooth sailing now that Tessa and I weren't fighting anymore and she was no longer trying to get her paws on Maiken. Plus, her attention was occupied now that she was dating Dustin again.

It seemed like every girl in school wanted to get her claws into Maiken. It was so hard not to get jealous.

"Trust in him," Momma had said. "Besides, sometimes it's hard not to notice something as blatant as a woman's breasts."

She had a point because even I'd been looking.

Celia jogged down the hall, her ponytail swinging like a monkey from branch to branch. Huffing and puffing, she skidded to a stop. "I found out who the new girl is. Her name is Sloane Price, and rumor is she was in juvie."

I'd hated to leave Maiken and Sloane alone the day before in the cafeteria, but I'd had a meeting with the guidance counselor. Because of that, I hadn't gotten a chance to find out any more about her. So I'd asked Celia if she knew anything. She hadn't at that time.

A laugh bubbled to the surface for some odd reason, maybe because I couldn't catch a break with girls wanting to get their hands on my boyfriend.

"You find that funny?" Celia asked.

"Hilarious." I wiped tears from my eyes. "You're probably going to tell me that she lives next door to Maiken."

Celia's rosy complexion paled.

"You've got to be kidding me." The Maxwell family owned all the land around the lake. In fact, they were probably the largest landowner in town aside from my parents with their farm.

"You know that house just before you turn down the road leading to Maiken's uncle's estate? She lives there."

Leave it to my best friend and reporter to find the dirt on someone.

"You're going to be a kick-ass reporter one day," I said.

"Did you just use the word ass in a sentence?" she teased.

I was finding that my shyness and aversion to swear words were diminishing down to nothing. I was also finding that I hardly stuttered anymore. I was blossoming, as my granny had put it.

"I'm growing," I said, pulling out my notebook. "I'm wiser and older."

She snorted and nudged me at the same time.

I glanced down the hall to find Ethan, Emma, Marcus, and Maiken strutting toward us. They had an aura that said, "Don't mess with us Maxwells."

The handful of girls congregating not far from Maiken's locker giggled. A couple of boys who were leaning against the wall outside a classroom ogled Emma. After all, Emma was beautiful. She had long, wavy brown hair, big brown eyes, and a body I would die for—tall, long legs, and curves that would make a mountain pass look inferior.

"I would kill for that body," Celia said as though she knew what I was thinking.

My eyes were riveted to my boyfriend. His weight-training regimen was sculpting his body in all the right places. He had bigger, more defined biceps, a broader chest, and abs that were hard and tight. I knew because I rubbed my hand up and down those hills and valleys every chance I had.

Celia leaned into me. "Do you think you and Maiken will have sex this year?"

I swallowed thickly. "I don't know. It's not something we talk about." I wasn't ready. I wasn't sure when I would be. Anytime I thought about sex, I got nervous to the point that I couldn't breathe. Maiken had seen me in my bathing suit, but my body wasn't what I was worried about. My head kept getting in the way.

"Question is, girl," I said as the Maxwell clan huddled at Maiken's locker, "when are you?" It was a nonsensical question since Celia didn't have a boyfriend. She was still hung up on my brother Liam, who was now a big-time senior with no girlfriend to speak of.

My brother Carter had graduated, thank God. I didn't need him raining on my junior year with his big-brother attitude. His absence was one reason I felt a little freer and had a higher self-esteem. He wasn't there to scare Maiken or any boy away from me.

Maiken was absorbed in talking to Marcus, who was strikingly handsome like Maiken. Two years separated them, and Marcus had perpetually unruly hair, but he had the bluest eyes on the planet like Maiken.

"We have maybe two minutes before the bell rings. I'll see you in class," I said to Celia. As I made my way toward Maiken, someone tugged on my sweater.

I pivoted on my heel and came face-to-face with Sloane Price. Normally, I didn't size girls up so blatantly, but I couldn't believe what she was wearing. Summer had come and gone. Sure, sometimes in New England, we got what meteorologists called an Indian summer, where warmer weather came out of nowhere. But the fall mornings had been and still were chilly and cool, not the type of weather for short shorts and a tank top.

"It's Quinn, right?" she asked.

My nose twitched as I narrowed my eyes. "What do you want?" *If she says Maiken, I'll deck her.*

Her glossy lips curled at the edges. "Just to talk."

I couldn't imagine what she wanted from me. Supposedly, Maiken was her tutor, but I still didn't know that story.

I hiked my purse higher on my shoulder. "About?"

A tall, lanky boy passed us, gawking at Sloane, or rather gawking at her cleavage.

"I need a job. I understand that your dad hires this time of year."

Someone bumped into me, so I slid out of the way toward an open classroom door. "You want to work on our farm?"

She followed me. "I don't live far, and why not? I understand you have horses. I love horses."

Daddy was hiring not only for the holiday season but for a ranch hand or someone who could take Carter's place now that my brother was attending Boston College. His decision had been a last-minute thing. He hadn't been sure what he was going to do after high school. But when he'd applied for a student loan and it was approved, Momma and Daddy had encouraged him to go.

"I'm not sure you could handle my dad." That was the honest truth. My dad didn't tolerate any employee who was trouble or brought trouble with them. And if Sloane had been in juvie like Celia had mentioned, that could pose a problem.

She curled a wad of her white-blond hair behind her ear. "Well, I'm going over there today." Her brown gaze drifted past me. "Ooh. I see Maiken. Isn't he hot as hell? His brothers too." Then she darted around me.

I wanted to scream. I wanted to knock some sense into her so she would know she couldn't just waltz into my school, start trouble, and ruin people's lives.

She isn't ruining anyone's life. Yes, she is. She just wants attention. Maiken's attention.

I schooled my features and started for Maiken. But when I did, the final bell rang. Not only that, he was walking away with Marcus on one side and Sloane trailing him.

It was official. Sloane Price was going to be the bane of my junior year.

Chapter 3

Maiken

I had a vision of me banging my head against the wall over and over again. I was tempted to do just that on the bookcases in the library. Sloane was late. I had better things to do with my free period than sit around and wait for a girl I didn't know, especially one who was trouble with a capital T. My physics teacher, Mr. Canwell, had asked me if I could show Sloane what she'd missed so far and to help her if she had any questions on the homework.

"Why me?" I'd asked him.

"Because she's your lab partner," he'd responded.

I couldn't say no only because my grade depended on her since we were lab partners, and lab was one third of my overall grade.

I texted Quinn while I waited. I'd seen her in the hall that morning, but Marcus and I had gotten into an argument, derailing any chance of grabbing a quick kiss from Quinn before the bell rang.

Where are you, baby doll? My girl had been ghosting me all morning. I understood that we couldn't use our phones during class, but in between was a different story.

As soon as I hit send, Sloane Price ambled in as if she owned the damn library. I had a feeling she was going to drive me to crazy land. It wasn't that she'd done anything specific. I couldn't put my finger on why she rubbed me the wrong way.

She slid into the chair across from me with a flair of attitude as though I were the one taking her away from something fun. "Let's get this party started."

Let's not and say we did. "I'll show you what you missed, then you're on your own."

"Not likely."

I cocked my head. "Come again?"

"We're lab partners, dude. So I need all the deets on what we're doing for lab too."

Fun times.

I opened my physics book. "So you're new here. Where did you live before?" Maybe if I made idle chat, the time would go quicker.

She gave me a cheeky grin. "Juvie."

I didn't react only because I didn't believe her. But I would bite. "What did you do?"

"Killed a man," she said seriously.

I studied her, from the hard glare in her eyes to her tiny studded nose ring that glinted in the light. She might have been in juvie, but not for killing a man.

"I'm not that easy," I fired back.

She sucked in her lips. "Too bad."

I rested my elbows on the table and leaned forward a little. "Let's get something straight. I'm helping you because Mr. Canwell asked me. So get your book out."

She slouched in her chair, not making any effort. "So, I'm having a party Saturday night. You want to come?"

Parties and I didn't jibe. "Nope."

"Shame," she said. "Your brother Marcus is coming."

I did a double take. Now she had my attention. "You're the girl he was talking about?"

Oh, hell to the no.

When Marcus had mentioned he was going to a party on Saturday night, I'd flat out told him he couldn't. That had been the crux of our argument at my locker that morning. It wasn't that I didn't want my brother to have a good time, but parties breathed trouble, booze, and who knew what else.

"I'll go with and keep an eye on him," Ethan had said.

Even Emma was all in, which didn't surprise me. My sister was all about parties. That alone scared me. I had a feeling I would become that overprotective brother like Carter Thompson.

"Marcus won't be going to your party," I said as sure as the librarian was eyeing me to lower my voice.

Sloane pressed her chest against the edge of the table and whispered, "He's a big boy, and you're not his dad anyway."

Inwardly, I cringed at the word dad. If my dad were alive, I wasn't certain if he would approve of Marcus going to a party or not. Regardless, Marcus was in a vulnerable state, and I didn't trust Sloane with my brother. I did think a girlfriend might bring him out of his rebellious and depressed mood, but if Sloane truly had been in juvie, she could very well encourage Marcus to do things that could land him in the same predicament.

"Stay away from my brother."

"Or what?"

Man, the girl was digging into my skin like a dog sinking its teeth in to feed.

"Where's your book?" I asked again.

She reluctantly unzipped her bag.

While I waited, I spied Tessa Stevens gliding toward us with questions written all over her face. She was another girl that rubbed me the wrong way, although I could tolerate her a tiny bit since she and Quinn were being cordial to one another now.

As Sloane placed her physics book on the table, she followed my line of sight. "I hear she's pregnant."

I rolled my eyes. The girl had only been at Kensington for two days at most, and she was already deep in the drama pit. "Not true."

Sloane casually lifted a shoulder. "Most rumors around school are true to some extent."

"Did you spread gossip around at juvie?" I mumbled.

Tessa stuck her hands on her hips, sizing up Sloane. "I saw you in the admin office yesterday. You're new here."

"Sue me," Sloan said.

Ignoring Sloane's barb, Tessa set her dark gaze on me. "Cheating on Quinn already?"

I couldn't tell if she was serious or teasing. Either way, I growled.

"He is," Sloane chimed in.

That vision of me banging my head against a wall surfaced, sharp and bright.

"Shut it, Price," I said loudly.

"Shhh," the gray-haired librarian said.

By the end of the day, the rumor around school would be that I was cheating on Quinn. Yep, it was time to blow this joint. I had two brothers to find. I had a girl that I wanted to see, and above all else, I wanted nothing to do with Sloane Price.

"Got to go," I said.

"Wait, what about physics?" Sloane asked.

"Read chapters one through four." I nodded at Tessa. "Good to see you." *Not.*

Then I sprinted out of the library and right into Quinn.

"What's the rush?" she asked in her sweet voice. "I was coming to see you."

"You have a class, don't you?" Why was I even questioning her? I didn't care if she had class or some other commitment. I was stoked to see those amber eyes that had a way of making me warm all over. And I couldn't get enough of those heart-shaped lips that I wanted on me.

"I took my calculus test. Then I asked to go to the library to study." Quinn peeked into the library through the slim rectangular window. "Tessa is talking to Sloane." Horror etched her tone. "Put those two together, and talk about double trouble."

I grasped her hand. "Come on. We have a few minutes. I know a quiet spot."

She didn't argue but hurried to catch up with me. "Where?"

"You'll see." I'd scoped out spots when school started up, knowing I might need somewhere for Quinn and me to steal a kiss or two.

Three halls and one door later, we were in a four-by-four room that housed boxes of old files. The odor wasn't all that great—it was musty and dusty. But with Quinn tethered to me and the scent of her vanilla-scented shampoo in my nose, I was oblivious to everything else.

Once the door was closed, I crushed my mouth to hers. She didn't complain. Instead, her hands went around my neck. I clutched her hips and lifted her up onto a stack of boxes. Our tongues danced while my hands slid up to cup her face. Kissing her was my favorite thing to do, even over basketball. I loved the game. I loved hearing the crowd cheer. I even loved the hard practices Coach and Kade put us through. But nothing in the world could compare to how I felt about this girl who was my everything.

Breaking the kiss, I pressed my forehead to hers. "Hi."

"Hi back."

"Did you get my texts?" I asked.

"Yep. All seven of them."

My heart raced. "And?"

She snaked out her tongue. "I'm the luckiest girl alive. I want to hear you recite the poem rather than read it."

I was shocked at myself that I could even write a poem. I'd struggled in English the previous school year to the point that I'd been failing. One assignment had been to write a poem. But I wasn't a poet, and I'd struggled with getting words on paper, especially words that when strung together would have meaning and maybe even rhyme. Then I'd watched Quinn skate around the lake that day. It had been magic when I'd taken pen to paper and the poem flowed out of me.

I swallowed what felt like an elephant. Anytime I wrote her a poem, my nerves sang.

Keeping my forehead against hers, I started reciting the poem I'd written that morning in English. "Your butterscotch hair shimmers in the light. Your amber eyes sparkle and ignite. Your lips"—I pecked her on her mouth—"are soft and taste like berry." I dragged my mouth up to her ear. "Nothing about our relationship is temporary." I pulled away so I could lock eyes with her. "I look at you like you hung the moon. And all day long, I swoon and swoon and swoon."

She sighed, smiling from ear to ear with so much love in her eyes, my knees became weak. I pressed my hands on the boxes on each side of her to keep my legs from buckling. I wasn't exaggerating. This girl did things to me that were out of my control, and for that, I had to take a step back.

She tracked my movements, her chest heaving.

Yeah, we both felt the same way about each other. We had a deep love and a strong bond that grew each and every day.

I pivoted on my heel, walked a few steps, then adjusted my jeans.

"It's okay," she said softly. "Our physical reactions are normal, Maiken."

Normal, yes. But my self-control was waning. Regardless, I shouldn't have been embarrassed. So I turned and leaned against the back wall.

Quinn giggled, her gaze on my crotch. Then her eyes slowly lifted to meet mine.

I cleared my throat. "I haven't officially asked, but would you like to be my date for homecoming?"

She squealed as she all but threw herself at me. "Of course. I've been waiting for you to ask. I know you don't like parties."

"I do if you're with me."

My response only made her press her body into me more.

Holy cow! If we stayed in the closet any longer, I couldn't promise I would be a gentleman. Being around Quinn with her body against mine, our tongues fused, and our hands all over each other was eroding my self-control.

"We should go." My voice was strained.

"First, tell me about Sloane," she said.

And just like that, my boner deflated.

Chapter 4
Quinn

The farm store wasn't busy for a Thursday afternoon in late September. Homecoming was three weeks away, and I had to find a dress. I sat behind the counter, searching store after store online for something simple yet pretty, a dress that would cause Maiken to do a double take when he laid eyes on me. I didn't have a ton of money to spend. Granny had given me a hundred dollars at Christmas that I hadn't touched yet. But all the dresses I liked were way over a hundred dollars.

I clicked out of one website and texted Celia.

Quinn: *Shopping Saturday afternoon for homecoming?*

Ashford had a local dress shop, and if I were lucky, I could find a dress on the clearance rack.

Celia: *Sorry, I can't. My parents and I are going up to Vermont to ski. Want to come?*

Quinn: *Momma wants me to work Saturday morning at the store. Besides, you know I don't ski.*

With October almost here, we needed to keep stocking shelves and the storeroom.

Celia: *Are you going to Sloane's party on Saturday night?*

Quinn: *No. I wasn't invited.*

Not that I was surprised. She and I hadn't started off on the right foot.

Maiken had told me all about Sloane. He didn't like that she was his lab partner in physics. He didn't like that she'd asked Marcus to go to her party. He felt she was trouble, and with her time in juvie, he didn't want her around Marcus.

And I didn't want her around Maiken.

The bell dinged on the door.

I looked up from my phone to find Sloane Price walking in.

She glanced around as though she were in awe with the myriad of displays we had scattered around of jams, honey, and other items like trinkets and winter hats and gloves.

I set my phone down on the glass counter and kept my eyes glued to her.

She tried on a gray knit hat with a large pom-pom on top. The hat didn't suit her white-blond hair or her snow-white complexion.

I was tempted to tell her that we didn't sell devil ears, which would have been perfect for her. But I'd been taught manners, especially when it came to customers.

She returned the hat to the display and moved on to the next table, which held handmade jewelry from a designer Momma knew in town. Sloane twirled the rack around, and the necklaces clinked together.

"Why are you here?" I finally asked. Then I remembered she wanted a job on the farm.

She laughed. "You know why." She went to the next display of jams and jellies. "I want to fill out an application."

"We're not hiring," I said. *Father Thomas will give you a high penance at confession for lying.*

She moved slowly around the store, checking out everything we sold. "That's not what the sign says on the door."

"My dad doesn't hire ex-convicts."

She stalked toward me, her red lips pressed together in a thin line. "Are you going to give me an application or not?" She settled on the other side of the counter from me with her chest out and her chin lifted. Everything about her screamed defiance.

Studying her, I slid off the stool. Instead of shorts and a tank top, she was standing before me in black jeans and a long-sleeved T-shirt that had the words "Dare to Live" scrawled across the front. The first thing that came to mind was the song, which was written by Kody Maxwell, one of Kade's brothers, and sung by Kody's girlfriend, Jessie Ryan.

She tapped on the counter. "Are you staring at my breasts, Quinn Thompson?"

I blinked, narrowing my eyes. "Do you like that song?" I pointed to her shirt.

"Are you going to give me an application? Or do I have to scour the farm to find your dad?" Her voice was sweet. However, her attitude was anything but.

I guessed it wouldn't matter if I gave her one. My dad wouldn't hire her anyway. Reluctantly, I pulled out an application from the drawer under the counter.

She grabbed a pen from one of the many we had in a cup next to the register, took the application, and moved off to the side. She hovered over the paper as she wrote.

I rolled my eyes even though she wasn't looking at me. Of course I would read it when she finished. "You said you like horses. Have you ever ridden?" I didn't know why I was making idle chitchat with her. She probably wouldn't give me a straight answer, or she would just not answer at all since she'd avoided my other two questions.

All she did was nod.

A beat of silence passed, and while still writing, she said, "I'm having a party Saturday night. You want to come?"

At the last party I went to, I'd ended up in a pool of ice water. Still, I'd never been to a teen party, and it had to be better than the holiday gala with adults.

Before I could answer, she stuck the top of the pen into her mouth and looked at me. "Your boyfriend is coming."

What! Maiken hadn't said he was going. All he'd told me was that she'd asked Marcus. "He doesn't like parties."

She pushed out her shoulders and continued to fill out the rest of the application.

I grabbed my phone and texted Maiken. *Are you going to Sloane's party on Saturday?*

I chewed on the inside of my cheek, waiting to see the three bouncing dots that indicated he was replying. But there was nothing.

I rifled through my brain to replay the conversation Maiken and I had had in the storage room at school yesterday morning. But I couldn't recall him saying anything about going to the party. Maybe I'd been too dizzy over the poem he'd written for me and recited, or we'd been too amped up on endorphins from our intense make-out session. Come to think of it, he'd never had a chance to finish telling me about Sloane before the bell had rung.

An older woman in her fifties came in and went straight to the refrigerators that lined the back wall.

Sloane set the pen down. "Is your dad here? I would like to give him my application personally."

I had to give Sloane props for not trusting me, not that I would tear up her application.

"Ma'am," the lady said. "Do you have any raw milk?"

I pocketed my phone then skirted the counter to help the woman. We should've had a few gallons, but upon inspection, I didn't see any. "Let me check. How much do you need?" Daddy kept reserves in the fridge in the back room.

"Two gallons," she said.

Just as I crossed the threshold from the store into the hall, the back door opened.

Daddy removed his ball cap and wiped the sweat off his forehead. "Sweet girl. Is it busy today?"

I stabbed my thumb over my shoulder. "We're out of raw milk?" I asked more than said. "We have a customer who needs two gallons."

He mussed his thick brown hair, which was matted to his head. "We have several in the storeroom. I'll get it."

I backtracked. "Ma'am, my dad will be right out with some." Then I returned to the counter.

Sloane set the pen down. "So your dad is here?"

At that moment, Daddy came out with two gallons of raw milk and carried them to the counter. "My daughter will ring you up."

The older lady followed, taking out her wallet.

Sloane cornered Daddy. "Mr. Thompson, I'm looking for a job." She handed the long piece of paper to my dad.

While I rang up the lady's order, Daddy read through Sloane's application, circling the counter to stand next to me.

The lady paid and left in a hurry.

Sloane leaned against the counter, watching Daddy while he scrubbed a hand over his jaw, reading.

"Is there anything I can answer for you, Mr. Thompson?" Sloane asked in a sweet voice. "I'm a hard worker."

"Your parents owned horses?" Daddy sounded surprised.

I was too.

"They did at one time." She sounded melancholy.

"Why do you want to work on a farm?" Daddy asked all applicants that question.

A farm was backbreaking work. Several people he'd hired over the years didn't last more than a week. Not only that, my dad was a tough man to work for.

She smiled. "I love animals, and I know the ins and outs of a farm since I lived on one."

My mouth parted slightly. A farm girl? I didn't see that coming. *Not all farm girls are shy like you.* Maybe I was trying to make sense of Sloane living on a farm and being in juvie.

The bell dinged, and Liam strutted in, beelining to the fridge, which was normal for my brother when he came into the farm store. Until he laid eyes on Sloane. Then he sidestepped, sizing her up. "What's going on?"

She swung her attention to Liam, batting her lashes. "Hi. I'm Sloane."

I refrained from another eye roll and a snarky remark only because my dad was there.

"Liam. Are you applying for a job?"

"She is," Daddy said. "But I have other applicants I'm considering. We'll be in touch, Ms. Price."

She frowned. "Any idea when?" She sounded desperate, which I found odd. The home she'd moved into was as big as the Maxwell mansion. That alone said her parents had money.

"I'll be making a decision next week," Daddy said firmly.

She thanked my dad then made her way out with a pouty expression.

Suddenly, I felt sorry for her.

"Is she new in town?" Liam's voice had a hitch to it. My brother was smitten with her.

Daddy placed her application in the drawer. "Moved in to the vacant house at the corner of Bradbury Road."

"That's the road to the Maxwell estate," Liam mumbled. "I might have to visit the Maxwells more often."

Daddy didn't react to Liam. Instead, he took some cash from the register. "I need to run into town. Once you close up here, both of you start your chores early." He swaggered off into the back room.

"What grade is she in?" Liam asked. "I haven't seen her around school yet."

"Junior. She's new at school, and she's been in juvie apparently."

His eyes were as shiny as a copper penny. "Nice."

"Not nice." I snagged her application. "Daddy won't hire her if she's been in juvie." It wasn't that I wanted my dad to give her a job. Although maybe it would be nice to have another girl around the farm, especially one who'd lived on one.

"She's cute," Liam said.

"You don't do cute."

"You know my type?" he teased.

"I know you're a prude when it comes to girls. Are you going to ask Celia to homecoming?" My BFF still had the hots for my brother.

"Or when are you going to find a girlfriend?" I couldn't force him to date Celia.

He grinned. "Who says I don't have one?"

"Oh my God. Do you?" He hadn't talked about one, and I'd never seen him with a girl.

"Nah. But hey. That might change now." He waggled his eyebrows. "Maybe Sloane will go out with me."

I should react or say something about Celia, but my brain was trying to make sense of what I was reading on Sloane's application.

Liam leaned his elbows on the counter. "What is it?"

"She checked no next to police record. Isn't juvie like jail?" I didn't know anything about juvie except that juvenile facilities housed underage kids who had broken the law.

"Maybe she wasn't in juvie," Liam said.

"She told Maiken she was." Plus, Celia had said the same thing.

"Maybe she lied."

If she had, then why? Regardless, I was obligated to share what I knew about the mysterious Sloane Price with my dad.

My phone rang, and Maiken's name came across the screen.

"I'm out of here, sis. I'll see you down in the horse barn." Liam faded from view.

I lifted my phone to my ear. "Hey."

"Do you want to go to Sloane's party on Saturday?" Maiken asked, sounding as if the party were the worst thing in his life.

"Sure." I would go anywhere with him.

"I have to babysit Marcus," he said. "Kade feels like the party might do Marcus some good. You know, get him socializing instead of fighting."

"Parties can be fun," I said. Maybe a party of our peers would be.

Maybe I could also find out why Sloane was lying. I doubted a party would tell me the truth, but it might reveal more of who Sloane Price really was.

Chapter 5

Maiken

When Ethan and I walked through the door of Sloane's house, music was blasting, kids were lined up on both sides of the foyer, and others were crowded into the large, open room to my left, dancing to some fast-beat tune. Even more people sat around a dining table in the room to my right, playing cards.

"Why did I come?" I asked no one in particular. Parties made me claustrophobic.

I shuffled in deeper, focusing on the bright lights ahead, which I assumed was the kitchen. Quinn was meeting me there, but I had to find Marcus first. He'd taken off without Ethan or me knowing.

You can't babysit him every minute of the day. You're going to drive yourself nuts.

I took some consolation in knowing that Emma had tagged along with Marcus. She would keep an eye on him. Or at least I hoped she would.

I kept telling myself he would be fine. He was probably talking with friends and having a good time. Kade's advice had been to let him enjoy himself.

Maybe it was my aversion to parties that had me all messed up.

Some kids nodded at me as they chatted and drank from red plastic cups. I would bet some of those cups had alcohol in them. And because of that, I tensed.

I tossed a look over my shoulder. "Find Marcus," I said to Ethan, who was right on my heels.

He darted into the dance room while I continued my quest into the spacious gourmet kitchen, where kids were laughing and talking over the music.

I barely had a chance to scan the room when Quinn came out of nowhere. She beamed up at me. Her cheeks were rosy, and a sheen of sweat covered her forehead. "There you are!"

For a brief moment, I forgot where I was as my gaze roamed up and down Quinn's curvy body. Her hair was wrapped up in a messy bun, a contrast to her normal style of letting it hang wild and free. Nevertheless, I was digging how her smooth skin was exposed all the way down to her formfitting top.

I swallowed thickly, taking in her stained pink lips and the way her thick lashes framed those big amber eyes I so loved. *Damn.* She looked lit, as the guys on the team would say when they saw a hot chick.

"You should wear your hair like that more often," I said in her ear. Maybe she and I should go to parties more often.

I could feel her smile against my cheek. Then her hands were around my waist until someone was pulling us apart.

I seriously was going to deck the person.

"Maiken, we need to talk," Sloane shouted as close to my ear as possible.

I had nothing to say to her. I'd barely said anything to her in physics class on Friday. Even during my free period when we'd met in the library, I had kept our conversation on physics and nothing more. I'd wanted to probe her on what her angle was with my brother Marcus. Apparently, she and Marcus had been sitting together at lunch the last two days. But I knew no matter how much I questioned her motives, she wouldn't tell me anything, and if she did, I was sure I wouldn't get the truth. Quinn had even mentioned that Sloane had avoided her questions.

Quinn cocked her head at me, silently asking what Sloane wanted.

"We have nothing to talk about," I said to Sloane. "This isn't physics."

Quinn tugged on my arm. "Emma is dancing. Come on."

Sloane dug her nails into my other arm. "It's Marcus."

My blood froze. "Where is he?"

She wagged her finger at the arched doorway that led to a hall then pushed through a crowd of kids blocking the exit.

My feet were moving superfast. My brain, on the other hand, was praying that nothing had happened to Marcus and that he hadn't beaten someone senseless. Fights were becoming the norm for my brother.

We traveled down a long, wide hall, passing closed doors, until we reached the end. A door on the left led outside, but instead of going out, which I assumed she would, Sloane waved her hand at the room on my right.

My pulse stuttered, and a boatload of fear pricked my skin. I was either going to find Marcus on top of a girl or bloody and beaten because he'd pissed off some brute. I inhaled, trying to get my heart-beat to stop punching my ribs, but when I laid eyes on Marcus, I couldn't breathe.

Quinn came to an abrupt halt next to me and sucked in a sharp breath. "Oh my."

I barreled in like I was being chased by a madman and knelt in front of my brother, who was swaying back and forth, holding his stomach while he sat on the closed lid of the toilet.

Fuck.

Blood dribbled out of a wound over his eye. He stank as though he had just taken a bath in alcohol, and he was a second away from passing out.

"What the fuck happened?" I asked him. "You're drunk?" Christ, none of us had ever touched any beer or alcohol.

"Bro," he slurred.

I whipped my head at Sloane, who was leaning against the outside door with an impassive expression on her face. "How did this happen?"

"Do you mean why is he drunk or what happened to his eye?" Her tone was a mixture of concern and go fuck yourself.

"Don't give me an attitude." I gritted my teeth. "Just tell me what happened."

Quinn snapped her fingers at Sloane. "Tell him."

Ethan appeared behind Quinn. His eyes were wide as he pushed his way in. "What the fuck?"

The bathroom wasn't big enough for Marcus, Ethan, and me.

"Get a wet cloth," I said to Ethan. "Sloane, where are your Band-Aids?" Marcus's cut didn't look like he needed stitches.

"Medicine cabinet behind you," she said.

"Quinn, can you and Sloane give us a minute?" Ethan asked politely.

I eyed Quinn and nodded. I didn't mind if she stayed, but this was family business, and no one else needed to see Marcus like that anyway.

When the door clicked shut, I growled loudly.

Marcus laughed. His eyes were heavy, and his skin was pale.

The urge to slap some sense into my brother was strong. But the act alone would do nothing to scare him straight.

Ethan wetted a hand towel. "Kade is going to be pissed."

I got some Band-Aids out of the cabinet. "I don't think so. He said to let Marcus have a good time. So this is what happens."

I was relieved that Mom wasn't living in Ashford. Seeing Marcus in this condition would devastate her, and she didn't need that kind of hassle right now. Plus, she might've been disappointed in me for not watching over him.

"The room is spinning." Marcus slurred the last word.

"We need to get him home," I said.

Before I could get out of the way, Marcus puked all over my boots.

I slammed my eyes shut for a second, hoping not to puke along with him, although my nerves were on the brink of destruction. High school was going to be a blast for the next two years.

We made quick work of tending to Marcus's wound then cleaning up the floor.

"Let's get him to the car," I said to Ethan. "Use the back door." Going through the house and dodging kids would be difficult carrying Marcus, and we didn't need people taking pictures or sending out viral texts about how drunk Marcus was.

Sloane was gone when we opened the door, but Quinn was biting a nail.

"I'm taking him home," I said to Quinn. "Sorry. Can you make sure Emma gets home?" My sister had walked to the party with Marcus earlier since Sloane didn't live far from the Maxwell estate, but I didn't want Emma walking home alone in the dark.

Nodding, Quinn opened the back door, which spilled out onto a deck. "I'll take her home."

After I gave her a quick kiss on the cheek, Ethan and I managed to drag Marcus around the house and get him into the car. Ten minutes later, we were helping Marcus up to his bedroom.

Voices from the TV floated through the main floor of Kade and Lacey's huge home. The two-story mansion consisted of six bedrooms, an office, a media room, a formal living room, a trophy and library room, a gourmet kitchen, four bathrooms, a game room, and a workout room. Apparently, they were expecting to have lots of kids running around the place.

Ethan and I lifted Marcus by his underarms, almost dragging him up one stair at a time. Marcus was deadweight as he drifted in and out of consciousness.

"Marcus." I tapped him on his face. "Help us."

He shook his head. "Spinning."

Oh shit. He was going to puke.

"Let's hurry and get him to the bathroom," I said to Ethan.

Ethan chuckled wryly. "He's heavy."

I glanced up. We had a long way to go around the curved staircase.

"Maybe we should let him sleep it off in the car," I said, feeling sweat bead on my forehead.

Ethan and I were strong. We both worked out. He had to keep in shape since he was playing football that year. I'd been working out, trying to keep in shape for the upcoming basketball season.

Ethan slapped Marcus on the face lightly. "Wake up, man."

Marcus jerked, and when he did, I lost my grip. All of a sudden, Marcus was sliding down the three steps we'd managed to climb.

Thud. Thud. Thud.

He hit his face on the stairs as he went.

Ethan threaded his hand through his hair. "There's no way Kade didn't hear that."

At least we didn't have to worry about Lacey since she was out of town.

We both scrambled to help Marcus, when heavy footsteps echoed. Then Kade was standing at the bottom of the stairs. His features were hard, his arms were crossed over his chest, and his eyes were narrowed.

"I told you it wasn't a good idea for Marcus to go that party," I said to him. I didn't mean to sound so harsh, but I knew my brother. *No. Scratch that.* I didn't know Marcus anymore. He'd always been a nice kid, obeying Mom and Dad.

But Dad isn't here anymore, and Mom is in Georgia.

I puffed out my cheeks, sighing so loud that I grunted.

Kade clutched Marcus's arm on one side. "Ethan, grab his other."

Ethan snapped to attention at Kade's command.

Marcus was like a rag doll as Kade and Ethan carried my brother around the staircase.

"Where are we taking him?" I asked.

"I'm going to do what my old man did to me when I came home drunk one time," Kade said.

I followed, guessing that Kade might pour coffee down Marcus's throat or stick his head under the kitchen faucet. That would surely wake up my brother.

But I'd guessed wrong.

Kade deposited my brother on a cushioned lounger out on the deck before he started barking orders. "Ethan, get a damp cloth. Maiken, grab a can of Coke from the fridge."

I didn't move from my spot at the accordion-style glass doors as Ethan blew past me.

Kade glared at me. "Coke, Maiken."

"Why did you bring him out here?" I trusted that Kade knew what he was doing, but I didn't understand why he didn't put Marcus in his bed.

Kade sat on the edge of the cushion as he ripped off the bloody Band-Aid over Marcus's eye. "Maiken." He said my name in warning. "Get a can of Coke."

Ethan returned and nudged me. "I got both." Holding the Coke in one hand, Ethan handed the damp cloth to Kade first.

Kade cleaned Marcus's wound. "How did he cut his eye?"

"Not sure," Ethan and I said in unison.

I was going to find out, though. I was also going to make sure Sloane stayed away from my brother. Marcus was the last person Sloane needed to befriend.

Kade held out his hand to Ethan, who in turn gave him the Coke. Then Kade tapped Marcus on the cheek. "Wake up. I need you to drink the Coke. It will help the nausea." Kade's tone was fatherly at the moment.

"I want to sleep," Marcus whined.

"Drink this first," Kade ordered again.

Marcus blinked several times as he raised his head. Kade held the Coke to my brother's mouth as though he were feeding an infant.

Marcus finally chugged the soda, burped, then closed his eyes once again.

Kade rose. "Now get some rest." His eyes flicked to Ethan and me. "You two follow me." His tone permitted no argument.

Suddenly, I felt like I was about to get punished by my dad, which sent a chill through me. Mom was tough on punishments, but Dad had been tougher. If Mom took away our TV privileges for a week, then Dad added a month onto it.

The chill coursing through me was also because I felt like I'd failed as a big brother. I felt like I'd disappointed my family. Plus, part of that chill was embarrassment. We were guests in my cousin's house. Kade had been nothing but welcoming and helpful to my family and me. He'd gone out of his way to step in as our guardian, and I had let him down.

"Are you going to let him sleep out there all night?" Ethan asked.

Kade washed his hands. "He'll stay out there for now. The cool air will help him. The two of you are going to watch him."

I ponied up to the marble island that was the centerpiece of the kitchen. "I don't understand. Why not just put him in his bed?"

Kade wiped his hands on a paper towel, searing me with his hard copper gaze. "As drunk as he is, I don't want him lying flat. People have been known to drown in their puke."

I'd heard of that, but I wasn't thinking along those lines.

"Where's your sister?" Kade asked.

"She wanted to stay," I said. "She's not drinking."

No sooner than Kade had mentioned his sister, Emma glided in. Her gaze bounced among the three of us. "Is Marcus okay?"

Kade tossed the paper towel in the trash. "He will be. We'll talk in the morning when Marcus is coherent. I'm going to bed. I expect you two to watch your brother." He wagged his finger between Ethan and me. "If he wakes up and is feeling fine, then you can help him to bed. Are we clear?"

All we could do was agree.

After Kade stalked out, I plopped onto a high-backed stool.

Emma checked on Marcus. "Why—"

"Don't ask," Ethan and I said in unison.

Ethan started to pull lunch meat out of the fridge. "Some party."

"Too bad you guys couldn't stay longer," Emma said, helping Ethan make sandwiches. "You missed a fight."

"Do you know what happened to Marcus?" I asked Emma. I could get mad at her for not watching him, but I was realizing that no amount of babysitting was going to help my brother. He was going to do what he wanted to do.

She spread mustard on the bread. "No. He and I split once we got inside. I did see him making out with Sloane, though, when I took a break from dancing."

I squeezed my eyes shut.

"Way to go, Marcus," Ethan mumbled.

"Sloane was passing out shots to everyone," Emma said. "I didn't drink, though."

I sighed. All of us were growing up, and experimenting was part of it. So I shouldn't have been so enraged at Marcus. I mean, Kade hadn't exactly freaked out.

"Is Quinn okay?" I asked.

Emma giggled. "A little shaken over Marcus, but she's fine. She believes Sloane is lying about who she is. I didn't get all the details. I could barely hear my own thoughts at the party." With her sandwich in hand, Emma started for the media room. "I'm going to watch TV."

When Ethan and I were alone, he sat down across from me and chomped on his sandwich.

"You can watch TV with Emma," I said.

"I'm not leaving you to watch Marcus. We're in this together, bro."

I loved my brother. I loved all my siblings, but Ethan and I had always been tight like Jasper and Marcus. Then it dawned on me. Maybe Marcus's rebellious nature stemmed not only from the death of Dad, but he was probably missing Jasper. After all, they'd been joined at the hip up until Marcus started high school this year.

I made a mental note to talk to Mom. Maybe having Jasper live with us would help to tame Marcus. Or maybe not.

Chapter 6

Quinn

Colorful leaves fluttered to the ground from the trees dotting the landscape around the church. Sunday mass had just let out, and adults were chatting with one another, catching up with friends and family. My mom and dad were listening to Eleanor and Martin Maxwell at the bottom of the church steps.

I wandered down the sidewalk a ways, looking at my phone. Celia had texted me during mass to ask about Sloane's party. She was bummed that she hadn't been able to go.

Quinn: *We'll talk when you get home.*

Celia: *We're on our way. Did you find a dress for homecoming?*

Quinn: *Negative. I'll wait for you.*

I hadn't had time to go shopping. Unpacking boxes of new items for the store had taken most of the day on Saturday.

Celia: *Great. I'll call you when I get home.*

My next call was to Maiken. I'd been worried all night about Marcus. I tried to find out what had happened to him after Maiken and Ethan had taken him home, but I'd struck out. The kids I'd spoken to before Emma and I had left Sloane's house didn't have a clue, although Emma had seen Marcus and Sloane kissing. But kissing hadn't given him that cut on his eye. He'd probably fallen if he had been as drunk as he'd looked.

I tapped Maiken's name on my phone. The line rang and rang until his voice mail picked up. So I sent him a text to call me.

No sooner than I had pocketed my phone, I spied Tessa walking toward me. She was dressed in a dark-red coat over a black dress, which matched her shiny black hair and dark eyes.

Not that long ago, I would've tensed or run when I saw Tessa. But everything between us had changed when she'd fallen through the ice back in January. We weren't friends that hung out, but we'd been friendly to one another. She didn't bully me anymore or anyone in school, for that matter. As head cheerleader, she had to set an example of professionalism, and bullying didn't fall into that category.

As for me, I didn't shy away from much anymore. My newfound confidence hadn't happened overnight, but gradually, day by day and week by week, I'd gained enough to stand up for myself.

She tightened the belt around her coat. "How was that party last night? I wanted to go, but Dustin had tickets to a preseason Bruins hockey game."

Dustin was a big deal at Kensington for the hockey team, much like Maiken was for the basketball team. Maiken was better-looking than Dustin in my opinion. I preferred clean-cut, sandy-blond-haired boys to unruly black-haired boys.

Shrugging, I checked on my parents, who were still deep in conversation with Eleanor and Martin. "Wild."

"I heard Marcus Maxwell got drunk and was out of control," she said.

Yikes. Word traveled fast for a weekend. I imagined pictures had been snapped and texts about the party had gone viral. "He was drunk, but I didn't see him out of control." I hadn't really seen him at all. I'd been dancing the whole time until Maiken showed up. "Two fights broke out, but that was after Maiken took Marcus home."

"Well, I hope to throw my own party around the homecoming dance. Are you going to homecoming with Maiken?"

"Yeah," I said even though it was a given.

"My brother is going to ask the new girl to go," she said. "Chase thinks Sloane is all that and a bag of tricks."

I snorted. I'd found that most boys at Sloane's party had been trying to get her attention. She was pretty, curvy, and showed off her skin for all to see. So I wasn't shocked that she'd turned boys' heads. As long as she didn't garner Maiken's attention, I didn't care.

"Speaking of Chase, I didn't see him at the party."

"He went skiing this weekend," she said.

So did Celia. My brain started making assumptions, but I discarded them. There were plenty of ski resorts in New England. Still, I asked, "Where?"

"Vermont. Why?"

"No reason." She would laugh if I told her what I was thinking. "I think Chase should ask someone else." Then I covered my mouth. "I'm sorry." I knew better than to judge a person.

Tessa's perfectly manicured eyebrows soared. "You care about my brother?"

I liked Chase enough not to see him with a girl like Sloane. He deserved someone sweet. "He's a nice guy, Tessa. He deserves a nice girlfriend."

She gave me an approving smile. "I hear she was in juvie."

"Do you know why?" I asked.

"I've heard several different reasons. So not really. I think people are speculating if you ask me." Her gaze drifted toward the church steps. "Your dad looks pissed."

I turned my head slightly and found she was right. Even though I hadn't done anything wrong, my nerves perked up as Daddy came toward me.

"Got to run." Tessa darted past Daddy and out to the parking lot.

Daddy tucked his hands into his pressed dress pants pockets. "Care to tell me what went on that party last night?"

Boom!

My heart stopped.

And I thought word got around school like wildfire. I suspected the

Maxwells had mentioned what had happened to Marcus to my parents. Unless my dad had heard about the party from Officer Daniels, who was now talking to Martin Maxwell.

"It was a party." I wasn't sure what else to tell him.

Daddy loosened his tie. "With booze, fights, and what else? Drugs?"

I swallowed the sand in my throat. I couldn't lie. I didn't want to either. My dad would ground me for the next two years if I so much as skirted the truth. More importantly, he wouldn't let me see Maiken anymore.

"The young Maxwell boy was passed out, drunk, and bleeding. Now start talking."

Yeah, I'd better, and I needed to start with me. "I didn't drink. I didn't see any drugs there. Two fights broke out, but that was after Maiken took his brother home. Maiken didn't drink either." I was quick to add the last part just in case he got any ideas that all the Maxwell boys were trouble. After all, he hadn't cared for Kade and his brothers when they were teenagers.

The whole town knew about the fight that had landed Kody Maxwell in a coma, and when the Maxwell boys retaliated, one of their rivals had ended up in the hospital. I'd only been eight years old at the time, but I remembered my parents talking about the Maxwell family. Daddy had used what had happened to Kody as a teaching lesson for Carter, Liam, and me.

In some ways, I thought I'd turned out to be the shy one because Daddy had put the fear of God into us about what would happen if any of his kids ever beat a person into a coma. Not that I wanted to beat anyone.

"I don't want you going to any more parties," he said.

I wanted to stomp my foot like a five-year-old. "Why?" That wasn't fair. "I didn't drink."

He scraped a hand along his jaw. "Quinn, parties only attract trouble. I don't want to see you get caught up with the wrong crowd either."

"You can't shelter me forever, Daddy."

"I'm doing this for your own good."

"Really?" I'd never questioned my dad. I'd never talked back to him either. "M-my good or y-yours?" Nerves were starting to get the better of me.

His lips flattened into a thin line. "Quinn, don't test me."

I'd been the only one out of Carter, Liam, and me who obeyed him when he laid down the law. Granted, my first party last year hadn't panned out so well for me when I fell into Tessa's pool in the dead of winter. But I wanted to have fun in my junior and senior years.

I sighed. "Daddy." Sugar laced my tone. "Trust me. I'm not going to get drunk or try drugs. You and Momma taught me responsibility."

He squeezed his temples. "I worry about you, sweet girl."

I hooked my arm in his. "I know. But I promise you—I will not touch alcohol or drugs." Honestly, I didn't care to. I wasn't like some of the kids at school who were dying to get drunk or drink beer or whatever.

We strolled back to Momma, who was just saying goodbye to Eleanor and Martin.

"Are you going to hire Sloane?" Considering he knew what had gone on at her party, maybe he would pass on her.

Daddy covered my hand with his rough one. "Between you and me, there's something about her that doesn't sit well with me."

Like father, like daughter.

"Word at school is she used to be in juvie," I said. "I know she didn't mention that on her application."

"I have ways of checking on people's backgrounds. Don't you worry."

Whether she worked on the farm or not, I firmly believed Sloane would be a thorn in my side.

Chapter 7

Maiken

I peeked into Marcus and Ethan's room through the door in our Jack-and-Jill bathroom. Ethan and I had finally gotten Marcus to bed about one in the morning. My brothers were fast asleep, and knowing them, they would probably sleep until late afternoon. At least Marcus would, considering all the alcohol he'd consumed.

I splashed water on my face, ran my wet fingers through my hair, then dressed in a pair of sweats and a T-shirt. Since it was Sunday, I wasn't sure what I was doing. However, I did know Kade would probably chew Marcus's butt off, and I had to be there for that. I grabbed my phone and made my way down the hall. The growling in my stomach was louder than the sound of my bare feet on the shiny new hardwood floors.

The sun's rays sliced in through the transom windows, touching my feet as I reached the banister that overlooked the foyer below. Hushed voices trickled up from halfway down the sweeping staircase. Since the house was brand-new, the stairs and floors didn't groan like in an older home. Regardless, I took my time, listening to Kade and Uncle Martin.

"Everyone at church was whispering about that party," Uncle Martin said. "Officer Daniels even knew about it."

I rounded the stairs and inched closer to the kitchen, stopping halfway down a small hall that served as the connection between the front and back of the house.

"We don't need more trouble. What you boys did as teenagers still doesn't sit well with some of the locals. If the kids are too much for you, your mom and I can take care of them."

"No, Dad. They need to have some structure. Moving around from home to home isn't going to help them. And let's not forget they're teenagers. Besides, Maiken was there to pick Marcus up."

A glass hit the counter, sounding to me like Uncle Martin put his cup down a little too hard. "I know you see a lot of yourself in Maiken. But he can't carry the weight of a family on his shoulders. He's got to grow up too. Look, son, maybe the kids need to talk to an expert like Kody did after Karen died. As you know, Dr. Davis even helped Lacey. I would talk to them, but I think someone other than family needs to."

Kade sighed heavily. "Kody and Lacey did only because they were ready to. Marcus is far from ready. If we force him, he'll only get worse. And no amount of yelling at him is going to work either. We need to continue to show him love and support."

"Christine needs to know what's going on," Uncle Martin said. "But you have to talk to Marcus. You can't just sweep this under the rug like it never happened."

"Christine has enough going on. Let me take care of this," Kade added.

I agreed with Kade. As much as I knew Mom needed to know, she didn't need more on her plate.

Silence ticked by for a few seconds. I was about to make my entrance when Kade spoke. "Do you know anything about the Price family that moved in up the road?"

"Jeff Thompson is working on finding out. Apparently, the daughter wants a job at the farm. So he's checking on things."

The doorbell rang.

Crap.

I hurried back the way I'd come, hoping not to get caught eavesdropping, but the figure looking through the slim rectangular window flanking one side of the front door saw me.

Oh well. I plastered on a smile as I answered.

My cousin Kody stood outside, grinning as though he knew what I'd been doing. "What's up, Maiken?"

I hunched my shoulders. "Not much." *Tons of shit.*

Trampling in, he stabbed his thumb out toward the driveway. "I see my old man is here. Everything okay?"

I raised an eyebrow at my cousin, who was two inches taller than me. "Why wouldn't it be?" If everyone at church knew about the party, then maybe the whole damn town did as well.

His blue eyes sang of mischief. "I was your age once."

Yeah, he knew.

He pocketed his keys. "Kade called me. I heard all about the party."

"Kody, is that you?" Kade asked loudly.

Kody started for the kitchen. "Yeah, man." Then he addressed me. "Are you coming? Or do you want to eavesdrop some more?"

Busted.

My uncle Martin, a Kade lookalike, was dressed in a sharp tailored suit, sitting on a stool, and holding a mug on the island in front of him. Kade was across from him, wearing a pair of tattered jeans and an untucked dark-blue button-up shirt rolled up at the sleeves.

I felt underdressed. Even Kody was dressed as though he'd gone to church. He wore a crisp shirt over black pants.

"Good morning." I busied myself, getting OJ out of the fridge.

Kody poured a cup of coffee. "Dad, what time is dinner tonight? Jessie is working a shift at the hospital until four."

Uncle Martin shook his head. "Why hasn't she quit? You both make good money with your songs?"

"She only picks up shifts when they need her and if she's free." Kody added milk to his coffee.

"Kody, are you still coming by the club this afternoon?" Kade asked.

They were talking like I wasn't even there. But that wasn't why I was feeling like I didn't matter. Kade and Kody were talking to their father, something I would never get to do again.

Standing in front of the sink with my back to them, I downed my orange juice and poured another as if the sweet liquid was hard-core liquor that I needed to erase the memories of my dad. But as their happy voices filled the kitchen, talking about Kelton and Kross, my other two cousins, I was on the verge of tears. Their family unit was tight. My cousins had a mom and dad, and they sounded like everything in their lives was perfect—something I was envious of and wanted so badly. I wanted perfect. I wanted my brothers and I to have the bond that my cousins had.

As I downed the last of the OJ, wallowing in self-pity, I caught sight of Marcus standing in the doorway.

Holy cow!

He looked like he'd gone several rounds in a ring. The cut on his eye was prominent on his pale skin, and his hair was wildly disheveled. If I weren't mistaken, I would bet he was still drunk.

I placed my glass in the sink and pivoted on my heel.

All eyes were on my brother. Uncle Martin, Kade, and Kody didn't move from their chairs.

Marcus padded toward me with his gaze on my uncle and cousins. "So is this where all of you yell at me?" One thing about Marcus was he wasn't shy at all. He attacked anything head on.

For the mere act of doing something to ease the tension, I poured him a glass of OJ.

He took the glass and settled his back against the sink like me.

"So let's hear your wisdom." Marcus's tone was scratchy.

My uncle and cousins didn't speak.

"I'll give myself the advice, then," Marcus said. "Did you learn your lesson? Not sure drinking was a lesson. How did you get the cut on your head? I stumbled and hit the corner of the fridge. Are you going to drink again? Probably. Any other questions?"

I slapped my brother on the arm so he would tone down his rude attitude. We'd been taught to respect our elders. Plus, if he kept challenging Kade, then our cousin might decide to kick us out. I had no problem moving to live with my mom, but I wanted to stay at Kensington.

Marcus whipped his head at me. "Don't you start either. I'm tired of hearing all your bullshit."

I snagged the OJ from him then shoved him out of the kitchen. "Get out of here."

Marcus charged me, tackling me to the tiled floor. My head narrowly missed the corner of the eight-burner stove.

He began punching me. "I hate you."

I didn't retaliate. If he needed to take out his aggression on someone, I would rather it be me.

But he only got in two punches before Kade was peeling him off me. Marcus fought Kade but had no chance of winning against his strength.

I pushed to my feet. "I think it's time we go live with Mom." Defeat rode my tone.

Marcus froze, his blue eyes getting as big as basketballs.

Kade held Marcus at arm's length while Kody stood behind my brother.

"What's wrong, bro?" I asked. "You don't want to move to Georgia?"

"Fuck you," Marcus shouted. Then he darted out of the kitchen. Within seconds, the door upstairs slammed shut.

Kody and Kade returned to their seats, seemingly unfazed by what had just happened.

Uncle Martin loosened his tie. "Are you hurt, Maiken?"

I fixed my T-shirt, which had gotten all twisted when I fell. "No, sir." I looked at Kade. "Do you agree that we should move to Georgia?"

"Take a seat." Uncle Martin pointed to the chair next to Kade.

I did as I was told. "I would like to say something, please." My tone was kind and respectful. "It's been hard for us since our dad died. I know all of you understand what we're going through. You've been so awesome in stepping up to help my mom. I agree with Kade. We can't keep moving around from here to Georgia and from house to house. I think Marcus is missing Jasper, though. They've been joined at the hip since they were little." I paused to let that sink in. I couldn't ask Kade to take in another sibling. He had his hands full with Marcus alone.

All three men looked at each other, not giving away any hint of what they were thinking.

I stood. "If we return to Georgia, can I ask one thing? Can we leave after homecoming? I want to take Quinn to the dance."

"When is homecoming?" Uncle Martin asked.

"In three weeks."

I didn't want to leave Ashford. I didn't want to leave Quinn. I felt like I'd been saying that every day since Mom had stayed in Georgia. Yet I would do what was necessary to help my family.

Chapter 8

Quinn

Sunday was turning out to be the best day of my life. I was at The Cave, the local nightclub in Ashford. I'd heard so much about the establishment since I was a kid. At one time, the club had catered to the teenage crowd—a place where local teens could listen to music, dance, and hang out with their friends. I couldn't wait to get into high school to come here. Sadly, the club was sold a few years ago to Lacey's dad, and now The Cave only allowed in adults twenty-one and older.

With a mechanical precision, I took in every nook and cranny of the club. Pictures of bands hung on the walls, Kody Maxwell stood tuning his guitar on the large stage, and a myriad of liquor bottles was displayed on the shelves behind the long L-shaped bar. But mostly, I was dying to try out the comfy sofas and chairs in the balcony.

"Can I go upstairs?" I asked Maiken, who was beside me, also scanning the club.

He answered by pulling me up the stairs. He'd been extremely quiet since we'd left Sloane's house. After he picked me up at the farm, we'd stopped by to talk to her. Maiken wanted to tell her to stay away from Marcus, but she hadn't been home.

No matter what anyone said, Sloane was her own person. She wasn't going to listen. I had a feeling Marcus wasn't either. Maiken had shared that he and Marcus had gotten into a fight that morning, which was evident from Maiken's split lip.

We commandeered two black plush chairs that were each big enough to fit two people.

Maiken sat on the edge of his chair, bracing his elbows on his knees. I only scooted forward in mine because the railing was in my way, and I wanted to take in the view.

Kody Maxwell, tall, handsome, and with blue eyes that reminded me of Maiken's, fiddled with the mic onstage.

When Maiken had called me to ask if I wanted to hang at the club, he'd mentioned that Kody wanted to test one of his new songs on teenagers.

"Where's your brothers and sister? I thought you said they would be here."

He pointed to the bar area.

When I refocused from the stage to where he was pointing, Marcus was walking in from a back room.

"Emma didn't want to come," he said. "And Ethan is lifting weights."

Marcus strutted over to the stage, appearing like he hadn't even drunk alcohol the night before. His hair was slicked back, the cut over his eye was covered with a small Band-Aid, and his eyes were as clear as Maiken's.

I sat back, watching Kade wipe stemmed glasses as he stood behind the bar, until Kody's voice rang through the speakers.

"Testing, one, two, three," Kody said into the mic.

Marcus dragged a chair closer to the stage. "So what I asked you earlier—will you do it?"

Kody sat down on a high stool, rested his guitar on his knees, and adjusted the mic near his mouth. Then he strummed a few chords. "Sure," he said to Marcus. "If you're serious."

Marcus straddled a chair, resting his forearms on the back. "I've always wanted to play the guitar."

Maiken stared at the stage, or Kody, or maybe Marcus, with a faraway look on his face. I knew he wasn't happy with his brother, but he hadn't been since school started. I had a feeling something else was bothering him, though.

Sloane came to mind, but I didn't want to bring her up. We were there to listen to Kody. Regardless, Maiken's tension and silence were becoming quite uncomfortable.

Tell him a fact. That always perks him up.

I reached over and took his hand. "Did you know that holding hands boosts love and bonding?"

He didn't grin, smile, or laugh like he usually did, and because of that, I got a queasy feeling in my stomach.

"I love you, Maiken." I hadn't said that to him in a while. We did love each other, but we didn't need to say it all the time. His actions and mine of hugging, holding hands, and kissing showed us how we felt about each other.

He turned his head slightly, and our gazes tangled. "You're everything to me, Quinn. Never forget that."

The tension I thought would ease sitting next to the love of my life only tightened. He sounded like he was saying goodbye.

I abandoned his hand and tugged on his arm. "What's going on?"

The sound of Kody's guitar filled the club.

Maiken bolted upright. "What is she doing here?"

It took me a second to refocus my attention while Maiken was barreling down the stairs at breakneck speed.

Sloane Price stared at the stage in awe. But she didn't get a chance to do much else before Maiken grabbed her arm.

She jerked out of his hold. "Ow. What are you doing?"

"You're not welcome here," Maiken all but shouted.

Kody stopped playing. Marcus rushed over to Sloane and Maiken. Kade, however, didn't move from behind the bar. I didn't even jump into action.

"Get your hands off her," Marcus snapped at Maiken. "You don't see me manhandling Quinn." Marcus liked Sloane. So did Liam and Chase. But Marcus had been the one kissing her according to Emma. "I invited her." Marcus glared at his older brother. "She's looking for a job, and Kade has an opening. I already cleared it with him."

Maiken raised his hands, backing away. "I'm done." He stomped off toward the bar instead of coming back upstairs.

Sloane was obviously adding to Maiken's foul mood.

I clutched my chest, debating how to help my boyfriend. I didn't think all the consoling in the world would help, although maybe a hug would. He'd told me not that long ago to never stop hugging him. He'd said that very thing when he found out that his aunt had stage IV breast cancer.

Marcus and Sloane went over to the bar. Sloane whispered something in Marcus's ear. He twitched, or maybe he shivered.

My eyes followed Maiken, who was getting a soda behind the bar. As much as I prayed Sloane was on the up-and-up and didn't take advantage of Marcus, she wasn't my concern at the moment. Sure, I wanted to know why she had lied on her employment application. But Maiken needed me.

I'd been so focused on the brothers that I hadn't heard or seen Kody coming up the stairs until he was sitting in Maiken's spot.

"That girl is going to either make or break Marcus," Kody said as a matter of fact.

"Speaking from experience?"

"Yep. I had that same drool when I laid eyes on Mandy my freshman year."

Kade and Maiken disappeared into the back room.

I focused on Kody. "What happened between you two?" Curious minds wanted to know.

"She died in a motorcycle accident."

I sucked in air. I didn't want to hear that. "Is that what you meant about Sloane making or breaking Marcus?"

"Oh God, no," Kody said in a rush. "I'm sorry. I didn't mean that someone would die."

I shivered nonetheless.

Marcus and Sloane were laughing with their backs to us.

"What I should've said is she's chasing something, and I think Marcus is a distraction for her."

Basically, she was using Marcus.

Sloane turned, glancing at the stage. It was then that the light bulb came on in my head. She was wearing the same "Dare to Live" T-shirt that she'd worn when she came into the farm store. She was using Marcus to get closer to Kody for some reason. Maybe she was a rabid fan.

"I think she wants something from you," I said softly.

Kody chuckled. "She wants to learn to play the guitar according to Marcus. He asked me if I could show him and her a couple of things. And she is a fan, more a fan of Jessie's than mine."

Maybe the puzzle pieces were coming together. But playing the guitar didn't explain why she'd lied on her employment application.

Chapter 9

Maiken

I hid in the old file room during my free period. That spot was my own little secret hideaway. I couldn't help but remember the makeshift cave Ethan and I had set up in our backyard when we lived in Texas. We'd been tikes, but we'd gotten the idea after we moved in. Mom had had a ton of big boxes that held hanging garments and other home items. We'd taken most of them and built a cozy cave-like place where we hid or played. Then the first hard rain had ruined it. Ethan and I had been devastated.

I flopped my head back, relishing in the solitude before my next class. I was sitting on the floor, sandwiched in between two tall stacks of banker's boxes. My back was against the wall, and my feet were planted on the floor with my knees pointing up toward the ceiling.

Three days had passed since Uncle Martin and Kade had given me their words of wisdom about whether they would send us to live with our mom. Uncle Martin had left the decision to Kade.

"I don't want to shuffle you guys around," Kade had said. "I'll handle things."

"Are you going to tell our mom what happened?" I'd asked.

"My dad and I decided it was best not to yet. She has a lot on her plate." Then he'd added, "Your point about Jasper is a good one, but it's too much for Lacey and me to take on more responsibility."

I couldn't blame him for that, and the more I thought about

Marcus, I knew Jasper wouldn't change him, not with Sloane in the picture.

At least for the moment, I didn't have to break any bad news to Ethan and Emma. Both were happy and making names for themselves —Ethan in football and Emma in volleyball. I was also relieved I didn't have to break Quinn's heart, or mine, for that matter.

I inhaled a few times then heard the door groan. I should have been worried that a staff member could find me in there, but frankly I didn't care. I swore if Sloane found me, I couldn't promise I would be nice. She'd been trying to talk to me in physics class, but I didn't want anything to do with her. It was bad enough she had snagged Marcus's attention.

I'd learned on Sunday at The Cave that Kody had agreed to show her a few things on the guitar. More than that, Sloane and Marcus had been all starry-eyed at one another, which was another thing that got under my skin. If she had been in juvie like she claimed, then I was afraid Marcus could end up there as well.

"Maiken." Quinn's whisper sent warmth through my body. "Are you in here?"

I hadn't been the best boyfriend in the last few days. I'd hardly talked to her, and I'd barely seen her. Yeah, I was avoiding my girl. I had thought she might seek me out or press me or text me nonstop, but she hadn't. She was probably giving me space. Regardless, I owed her an apology. She'd done nothing wrong except love me.

She came around the stack of boxes. Her hair was up off her neck. She'd been wearing a messy bun since I told her I liked it up. She pursed her glossy lips. "Please talk to me."

I patted the space between my legs.

She inched over, looking almost afraid to sit down, but she crossed her legs underneath her and scooted as close as she could.

I cocooned her with my legs and arms. "I'm sorry I haven't been talkative."

She batted her long lashes. "I know. I've been trying to give you some space. Is Marcus still acting out?"

"Not this week."

Her eyes shifted left then right, as though she were deciding if she should tell me something. I was onto her little habits. Anytime she was nervous about saying something, she either looked away or studied me. "So I'm not sure if I should tell you this. Actually, I haven't said anything to anyone. I overheard my dad talking to my mom."

All I could think was that her dad was sick with some type of disease that wasn't treatable. "Is your dad okay?"

She shuddered. "Yes. Yes, of course. It's not about my dad but Sloane."

I pressed my spine into the wall. "Did she murder someone?"

Quinn's face scrunched as her cheeks reddened. "Where did you hear that?"

"She told me, but I didn't believe her. Is it true?" I had to warn Marcus. I had to warn everyone in my family.

"No!" Her throat bobbed. "Promise me you won't say anything to anyone."

"Scout's honor."

She sighed. "My dad talked to Sloane's mom. She came into the farm store yesterday. Anyway, Daddy asked her about Sloane and if she'd been in juvie. Mrs. Price confirmed that her daughter was never in juvie."

"What? Why would she tell people that?"

Quinn hunched her shoulders. "Don't know. But she spent some time in a mental health facility in the Berkshires according to her mom, who confided in my dad. That's why you can't tell anyone. My dad would kill me if he knew I spread that around."

"Holy shit," I said. "I don't know what to make of that. Why was she in? Did you hear that part?"

"No. I feel sorry for her."

I didn't know how I felt about that. "Is your dad going to hire her?"

"Not sure. But she's dying to work on the farm. She used to live on one. Her mom thinks it would be good for her."

"She was a farm girl?"

Quinn poked me. "You got something against farm girls?"

I leaned in. "I love my farm girl."

"You're lucky you said *my* farm girl. If you kept it generic, I would hurt you."

I chuckled. It had been days since I'd laughed. Then I mentally slapped myself for wallowing in my own misery. Quinn always made me feel happy and forget that I had problems. "I know at The Cave last Sunday you were trying to make me feel better. Thank you. And thank you for making me smile today. I love you, Quinn Thompson."

She blushed. "So can we kiss and make up."

"Make up? We didn't fight."

"Let's say we did and make up."

A laugh rumbled out of my chest. "We don't need a fight to kiss."

She gave me one of her pouty, shy smiles. "Then what are you waiting for?"

I didn't need any more coaxing.

Chapter 10

Quinn

Celia dashed into the cafeteria just as I was sitting down at our normal table tucked into the back corner. My lunch period and Maiken's overlapped by a few minutes. I thought I would catch him, but as I scanned the packed room, I didn't see him. He normally sat at the same table as Celia and me.

Celia huffed out a breath, slinging her bag over the back of the chair. "You're not going to believe this. Liam asked me to homecoming."

I squealed as equal parts happiness and shock blanketed me. My brother had given me no indication. I guess he wouldn't. We didn't talk much about who he liked, although he thought Sloane was hot.

I clapped my hands. "Shopping this weekend, then." I still hadn't found a dress.

Celia had a permanent smile on her face as her espresso eyes danced with all kinds of joy. "For sure. Where's Maiken? He's usually here waiting for you before his lunch period ends."

I did one more scan but came up empty. "He's probably in the weight room." *Or our secret hideout.* He'd been there most of the week during his free period and sometimes at lunch.

Celia's phone beeped. She gave it a couple of taps, and her expression turned dour.

"What is it?" She normally got texts all day long since she worked for the school's newspaper. Kids would send her pictures of what was happening around school, even though Celia covered sports for Kensington.

She slid her phone over to me.

I squinted at the picture. "Is that Maiken?" I couldn't really tell with the kid on top of him punching him. The color drained from me. Aside from fighting with Chase during a basketball game last year, Maiken had never been in any trouble at school.

"They're in the gym," Celia said. "Let's go."

I didn't get a chance to even stand before Tessa stomped up to our table out of nowhere and slapped me so hard across the face that my head whipped in the opposite direction. Tears shot out unexpectedly. Instantly, I touched my face, too stunned to return the gesture.

Celia, on the other hand, jumped up and pulled Tessa by the pony-tail. "What do you think you're doing?"

I moved my jaw from side to side and opened my mouth wide to stretch my skin, hoping the pain would subside.

Everyone in the cafeteria froze around me. Aside from the food line where the servers were changing out metal pans of food, a pin drop could be heard.

"Who's the bully now?" Tessa snarled as her eyes filled with tears.

Celia let go of Tessa but didn't move from her side.

"I-I have no idea w-what you're talking about." I honestly didn't.

Celia tugged Tessa over to a chair across from me. "Sit."

Tessa squirmed to get out of Celia's hold, but my BFF was not having any of it. "I'm not a dog."

"Pfft," Celia said calmly. "Rabid dogs attack like you just did. So I would say you need to be commanded like one."

The kids at tables as far as I could see were cemented to us. Some even had their phones out.

Figures.

I rubbed my cheek, feeling a ridge and a small amount of... I pulled my finger away to find blood. Anger burned through my stomach. In all the years I'd known Tessa, she had never been angry enough to cause physical harm. Her way of hurting someone was with her words.

Celia examined my face. "It's a small scratch."

It might've been small, but it stung like wasps had just feasted on me.

Celia glowered at Tessa. "Start talking." Her tone was curt.

Tessa inhaled deeply, not taking her eyes off me. "I thought we were getting along. Why would you spread a rumor like that about me?"

I laughed, but it was not a nice sound. "I don't spread rumors. That's your d-department."

Tessa shook her head and kept shaking her head as tears began to flow hard and fast, messing up her mascara.

Celia flailed her arms at the audience. "It's all good. Go back to what you were doing."

No one moved.

Celia fumed. "Or else I'll make sure every one of you make the paper's gossip column."

Her threat did the trick, and everyone went back to eating or whatever they'd been doing before Tessa came in and went all crazy woman on me.

Celia dragged a chair to the end of the table in the aisle as though she were head honcho. She was in my book. At least she was at that moment. "Talk, Tessa."

Mr. Canwell, the physics teacher, stalked our way. "What's going on here?" He regarded me with concern in his green eyes. "Your face is rather red on one side." Then he addressed Tessa. "Is everything okay, Ms. Stevens?"

I was the one that got slapped, and he seemed more concerned with Tessa because she was sniffling.

"We're fine," I said. I didn't want to go the principal's office. I'd never been in trouble at school, and I wasn't about to start. Daddy would be livid if he had to come to school because I'd gotten into a fight.

Mr. Canwell lifted the cuff of his long-sleeved plaid shirt and checked his watch. "Lunch period is almost over. I suggest both of you clean up before heading back to class."

"We will," Celia said.

He sauntered off in the direction of the main doors.

I lightly dragged a hand over the cheek that Tessa had slapped. "Tessa, talk."

"There's a rumor going around school that I'm… I can't even say it. But I heard you were the one to start it." She pierced me with a glare.

I held out my hands, palms up. "What? I don't know what you're talking about."

She narrowed her eyes and studied me. "You really don't. Do you?"

Celia snapped her fingers. "Just say it already."

Tessa leaned in. "The rumor is I'm pregnant."

For the second time in a matter of twenty minutes or so, I was rendered speechless. In fact, my limbs were locked in place. I tried to get my tongue to come unglued from the roof of my mouth or clear the pebbles of sand stuck in my throat.

"Are you?" Celia sported the most stony-faced expression that I'd ever seen on her.

"Heck no," Tessa blurted out in a rush. "I haven't even given my V-card to anyone."

"How do you know it was me who spread that around?" My stomach was ready to heave either acid or maybe the eggs I'd had for breakfast that morning.

My mind scrambled to figure out why someone would spread that rumor and, more importantly, make everyone believe I was the one who'd done it. I didn't have any enemies. Tessa had been my only nemesis, and that was in the past.

She pulled out her phone, tapped on the screen, and held it in my face.

It was a picture of a mirror with words scribbled in red lipstick—Tessa Stevens is pregnant! Quinn Thompson.

My vision blurred slightly. I blinked several times to clear it. "I swear I didn't write that."

Tessa regarded me with a grimace. "You did threaten to spread that rumor last year if you recall."

I gulped down air, remembering that day in the gym after the basketball game when she'd been a witch. I had said, "I could tell everyone your ex got you pregnant last year." But I'd only said that to get under her skin.

"You know as well as I do I only wanted to make you mad," I said.

Celia reached over and touched my hand that was lying on the table. "Are you okay?"

I started bouncing my leg. "I'll be fine." *Liar.* The last time I had an anxiety attack was first day of high school, freshman year. I'd been so overwhelmed and scared of what to expect that I could hardly breathe. I'd had to sit in the nurse's office for an hour that day.

Barb's voice suddenly blared through the overhead speakers. "Tessa Stevens and Quinn Thompson, please report to the principal's office."

My blood gelled.

Tessa turned ashen.

Celia's eyebrows flew to her hairline.

I would be surprised if I didn't pass out between the cafeteria and the admin office. Nevertheless, I used the table as my anchor to stand.

Tessa hiked her bag over her shoulder. "Great. Principal Sanders will call my parents."

All I could think about was Daddy shouting and taking away my privileges, like seeing Maiken.

"Go," Celia said. "I'll find out who did this."

I gave her a weak smile. "Does it matter?" Whoever did it wanted to start trouble. Who knew what her motive was? I suspected the culprit was a girl.

Whispers and hushed voices tittered as Tessa and I walked out of the cafeteria. I should've been used to people talking about me. I should've been hardened by all the rumors Tessa had spread about me, but I wasn't.

The closer we got to the admin office, the more my stomach churned and my vision blurred. I was working toward making valedictorian. With this strike against me, that might not be possible. I had to have a perfect record.

Tessa mumbled to herself as her legs ate up every bit of floor between the cafeteria and the admin office. I actually trailed her only because I didn't want to rush to my own demise. I was probably making a big deal out the situation, but I could get into trouble for defacing school property.

But you didn't do it. Even though that were true, I didn't know how to prove it wasn't me. My name was written on the mirror.

Tessa swung open the glass door and stormed into the admin office, right up to Barb, Principal Sanders's assistant.

I managed to slip in before the door shut.

"Quinn?" Maiken's voice hitched.

I turned to my right and found Maiken, Marcus, and some beefy, sweaty guy sitting in chairs along the sidewall just outside of the principal's office.

It took me a moment to remember that Celia had shown me a picture of a guy punching Maiken—the same guy who was in a chair next to Maiken. All three boys were bloody around their mouths and noses. And Marcus had blood on the old wound he'd gotten at Sloane's party.

Maiken came over, his blue eyes examining me. "Who hit you?" He pinched my chin with his fingers and turned my face to one side. "Is this why you were called here? Tessa did this?" His tone was high.

I could ask him why he'd been in a fight, but I didn't really need to with Marcus in the admin office. It was clear that Maiken had probably been trying to break up a fight, defend his brother, or both.

"Long story," I said. I didn't want to go into it right then, and I couldn't if I wanted to because Kade walked in.

He took one look at Maiken and Marcus then went up to Barb. He had no expression and gave no indication he was mad at his cousins.

"Hi, Kade," Barb said in a mousy tone. "I'll let Principal Sanders know you're here."

I found one empty seat left beside Tessa as Maiken returned to his in between the burly boy and Marcus.

Never in a million years did I think I would be waiting to see Principal Sanders to get reprimanded.

Chapter 11

Maiken

I ran my tongue over my split lip while I fixated on Quinn. I didn't see bruises or blood on Tessa, but Quinn had a scratch mark like someone had swiped a sharp nail down her cheek.

Principal Sanders came out of her office and motioned to Kade. "Maxwells?"

I tapped Marcus on the thigh. He wasn't in any better shape than me. The old wound above his eye had opened, and dried blood was caked under his nose. Like me, he wasn't in any hurry to get yelled at or suspended. I suspected that might be his punishment, considering he'd been in the principal's office once before.

I gave Quinn one last look before I entered the spacious office even though I felt as if I were walking into a prison. The cozy room did nothing to take away the nausea in my stomach, and neither did the sunlight raining in behind the large mahogany desk with motes floating in the rays.

Marcus and I stayed just inside the office, near the loveseat. His head was down, his hands were tucked into his jeans pockets, and he shifted from one foot to the other.

I wanted to hug him. I wanted to tell him that he would get through whatever hell he was living in. But I couldn't. In his state of mind, he wasn't ready to hear that everything would be okay, that he would get over Dad's death, or that at least the pain would subside over time. I would be lying if I said all that right now because my pain for Dad hadn't gone away. However, basketball helped take my mind off of him, my aunt, and my mom. Having someone to love helped even more.

I swore that fate had thrown Quinn and me together for a reason. She was my rock. She was the person who helped me in more ways than she even knew. I wanted to believe that Sloane was the gal for Marcus, the one who would help him through his pain. But given that she'd been in a mental health facility, I suspected she had her own to deal with.

Principal Sanders crossed the room, her high heels clicking on the tiled floor. Kade followed her in and shut the door. His body was tense, his expression still and impassive. I had no doubt that after this meeting, Kade wouldn't want us living with him and Lacey anymore. I still hadn't told Quinn. I should have when she'd found me in the storage room on campus two days ago. But between wanting to forget my troubles and hearing the news about Sloane, I'd put moving out of my mind.

Principal Sanders sat down in her rich leather chair behind her expensive desk. "Boys, have a seat. Kade, you can bring the one near the loveseat closer."

"I'll stand," Kade said.

I nudged Marcus with my elbow. "Come on."

As much as I didn't want to sit, I did anyway. After I got out of there, I was going for a run. I'd been running every day after school, but after this, I was going to add two more miles to my run.

Once Marcus and I were seated and Kade had settled behind us, Principal Sanders spoke. "I'll get right to the point. I have a three-strike rule. Marcus, you've been in here twice already. So if you have one more incident, then I'll suspend you for a week." She clasped her hands in front of her. "Maiken, I hear great things from your teachers and Coach Dean. Honestly, I'm quite disappointed to see you here. But as I said, three strikes. This is your first."

"You're not going to ask us what happened?" I asked.

"I don't need to," she said. "You were fighting." She circled a finger around my face. "The evidence doesn't lie."

"But we didn't start it," Marcus shot out in a tone so angry, his face reddened.

She sat back, studying us with her stormy-gray eyes. She probably didn't believe my brother since he had a record of fighting.

"And you're lucky you didn't," she said. "Hence why I'm giving you a warning. If you had started the fight, there would be no warning."

"So you expect us to walk away when someone throws a punch at you or pushes you?" I asked.

Marcus jumped up, his messy hair falling over his eyes. "It makes no difference. I'm guilty no matter what." Then he stormed out.

"Explain what happened," Kade said.

I sighed. "Marcus and I were in the gym during lunch. He and I were shooting baskets. Then that kid, Ian, came in and just went off on Marcus. Something about how Marcus didn't own this school." I really didn't know the whole story yet. "Then Marcus told him to back off, but Ian pushed him. I tried to intervene, and Ian did this to me." I pointed to my split lip. "After that, Marcus tried to pull Ian off me, and you know the rest."

"Ms. Sanders," Kade said. "You've been the principal here for a long time, and I understand your rules." He grinned. "I lived them. But I'm asking you to give Maiken and Marcus a break. Their father's death is still very fresh, and Marcus needs to feel like someone has his back. Someone other than his brother."

Her features softened. "Kade, I can't relax my rules. If I do for one student, then I have to for all students. But given that Maiken here has not been in my office for any trouble—although that stunt on the basketball court last year should've gotten you suspended from school and not just games—I'll remove the strike from Maiken's record as well as Marcus's." She grabbed a pen that was lying on a folder and scribbled something down on a legal pad. "We're a month into the school year, and Marcus has been in two fights already. I hope for his sake he stays out of trouble."

"Thank you." I would've taken the strike for my brother. Sure, he was shredding my nerves, but he wasn't at fault that day. He and I had been enjoying a little brotherly time together, talking about sports mainly and how he was thinking of trying out for the hockey team.

That day had been the first day in a long time where Marcus acted like the Marcus I'd known before Dad died.

She held up her head. "Don't thank me. Thank him." She stabbed a red-painted nail at Kade. "It would do you and your siblings good to listen to that man. If anyone has experience with bullies, it's him."

Kade just stood there with a deadpan expression.

"You may go, Maiken. Kade, can I have a word with you in private?"

Kade nodded at me. "I'll see you at home."

"Principal Sanders, can I ask why you didn't suspend me from school last year?" Coach had benched me for three games, but I'd never thought about getting suspended from school.

"You can thank Coach Dean," she said.

I made a mental note to do just that as I left her office.

The sound of Barb's fingers on the keyboard echoed in the admin office. Quinn and Tessa were still sitting in the same two chairs, not saying a word.

"Mr. Maxwell," Barb said. "Take the late slip with you to class."

I didn't want to take any slip—I wanted to take Quinn and bolt. The fear on her pretty face made me want to hug her and tell her everything would be all right. But school wasn't out for another three hours, and if I skipped my afternoon classes, then I would definitely get a strike on my record.

I grabbed the slip then dropped into the empty chair next to her. "What happened?"

She picked at her nails.

Tessa shoved her phone in my face. "This is what happened."

I studied the picture of the mirror—Tessa Stevens is pregnant!

Quinn Thompson. I shouldn't have snorted, but I did. I couldn't help it. "Quinn didn't write this. Why would you think she did?"

Tessa gave me one of her bitchy smirks. "Are you forgetting we were enemies?"

"*Were* being the key word," I shot out. "You of all people should know that Quinn doesn't start rumors."

She lost her attitude. "I'm sorry, Quinn, for slapping you."

Quinn brought her fingers to her face. "I think I might've done the same thing if that rumor was about me. I just hope the principal believes me. Otherwise, I'll get suspended for defacing school property."

I clutched Quinn's hand. "I'm sure the principal will believe you. So, Tessa, is the rumor true?"

"Of course not, jerk face."

"I didn't believe it when I heard it last week, but I had to be sure."

Both girls sucked in air.

"What are you talking about?" Quinn asked.

"Sloane Price told me that last week. I told her it wasn't true."

Quinn and Tessa swapped a wide-eyed look.

Tessa got up and turned her back to Barb. "Sloane Price told you this?"

I handed the phone back to Tessa. "That's what I said."

As if what I'd just said was the key to erasing the animosity between Tessa and Quinn, they smiled at one another.

"Mr. Maxwell, get to class," Barb said.

I kissed Quinn where Tessa had scratched her. She didn't tell me Tessa had done it, but I knew. "We'll talk later."

"For sure," she said. "Marcus looked extremely mad. Are you guys suspended?"

I stood. "No."

But we might be moving after today. I wouldn't dare voice that concern out loud, but given what had happened, I was sure Kade was fed up with us.

Chapter 12

Quinn

L iam parked in the lot outside the farm store. "So who started the rumor about Tessa?"

"I don't know. But I'm going to find out." Someone was out to get me, and I believed Sloane was the culprit, especially after what Maiken had told Tessa and me earlier in the principal's office. But I was having a hard time understanding why Sloane would spread that rumor or why she would tell people she'd been in juvie when in fact she hadn't.

Liam killed the engine. "At least Principal Sanders believed you."

I was relieved, grateful, and thankful that I had a great track record at school with teachers and staff. My stomach had been in one big knot just waiting to see Principal Sanders, so much so that I could hardly look at Maiken. In the end, though, my record remained clean. She hadn't called my parents, and the biggest surprise of all was that Tessa and I had actually hugged each other after we'd left the principal's office.

"So Tessa isn't pregnant?" Liam asked.

"She's not, and I believe her." I did because Tessa had a future in ice-skating. She might even compete in the Olympics one day. She wouldn't throw that all away.

Despite that, the only reason Tessa had been called down to the admin office was because if the rumor were true, Principal Sanders wanted to find counseling for her.

"Being pregnant in high school is something that's hard to deal with," Principal Sanders had said.

I couldn't imagine dealing with a pregnancy as a teenager.

I clutched the door handle. "Please don't say anything to Mom or Dad. I don't want to worry them." They had been through enough over the years with Tessa bullying me. They didn't need to know someone else was out to get me.

Liam and I climbed out of the truck, and he came around to my side. "My lips are sealed. But it might be hard to hide with that scratch on your face."

I touched my face. *Argh!* I'd forgotten all about it now that the pain had gone away. My brain scrambled to find an excuse I could tell my parents, but I was coming up empty. I couldn't lie to them anyway.

"I'll cross that bridge if they ask." I was sure they would.

We went into the farm store, and Liam headed directly for the fridge as usual. But I stopped in my tracks when I saw Sloane and Daddy talking at the counter.

"What's going on?" I asked.

Sloane turned. Her white-blond hair was almost invisible against the bright light spilling in through the window behind the register. "Your dad just gave me the job." She was lit up like a Christmas tree. I'd never seen someone so excited to work on a farm.

Liam, who was opening a carton of milk, choked. "For real? You're going to work on the farm?"

I hadn't shared with him that I thought Sloane had spread the rumor about Tessa. Nor had I told him that Sloane had never been in juvie. I'd only shared that info with Maiken, who I trusted not to say anything. But I knew Liam's surprise was because he liked Sloane.

"You're taking Celia to homecoming. Aren't you, Liam?" I asked, hoping to shake the cobwebs from his brain and clear the dodo eyes he was sporting for Sloane.

I couldn't blame him in a way. Sloane was dressed in skinny jeans, hiking boots, and that "Dare to Live" T-shirt that I swore she wore every day.

Liam blinked then went about his afternoon routine of drinking milk and finding something to snack on.

Daddy came around the counter and kissed me on the forehead. When he pulled away, he examined my cheek. "Did you scratch yourself?"

"Dad, I'll show her around if you want," Liam said.

I held my breath.

Daddy regarded Liam. "Your sister will."

Not breathing yet, I waited for Daddy to ask about my cheek again. But he got his keys out of his jeans pocket. "Sweet girl, show Sloane the ropes. She can help you today down in the horse barn too. The horses need their bedding changed. We didn't get to it this morning."

I quietly released the air in my lungs, although I would tell Daddy the truth if he asked me about the scratch again.

"Tell your mom Liam will work in the farm store until closing. I'm headed into town for a bit," Daddy said.

Liam protested. "I can work in the barn."

Daddy grinned as though he knew Liam's motive. "Son, there'll be plenty of chores left when the store closes." Daddy removed his ball cap from the back pocket of his dirty work jeans and covered his head as he walked out.

Liam sauntered over to the counter, chewing on something. "You're welcome, sis."

I grinned at my brother. Since Carter had left for college, Liam and I were growing closer. I mean, we were already close, but Carter and Liam were two peas in a pod.

"Let's go," I said to Sloane.

"You sure you don't want to switch places?" Liam asked. "I did have your back."

"Why didn't you want to tell your dad about that scratch," Sloane asked innocently. "How did you get it?"

While it was none of her business, I was a bit surprised she didn't know. The majority of the school knew, at least the ones that had been in the cafeteria.

Liam sat on the stool near the register. "You must've heard."

She shook her head slightly. "I left at lunch. I had a doctor's appointment."

Whoever had written the rumor on the mirror had done it before lunch. So she still could've been the guilty party, although I was getting the vibe that she didn't do it since she seemed surprised.

"We should get down to the barn," I said for nothing more than to get my mind working again.

We left Liam and headed down to the house along a winding path with rolling hills on both sides. The sun slid down in the west, and a cool breeze ruffled my hair.

"It's pretty out here." Sloane sounded like a little girl who was remembering a time when she'd lived on the farm.

"What was your farm like?" I asked.

Her shoulders rose to her neck. "Not as big as this one."

I waited for her to tell me more, but she got a faraway look in her eyes.

When we approached the house, I slid my backpack off my shoulder and into my hand. "I need to drop off my bag. Do you want to come in?"

"Is it okay if I meet you down there?" Her tone was light and sweet, which was a stark contrast to the snarky voice and attitude she usually had. It was as if the farm had injected her with some kind of sweet juju.

"I'll be a few minutes. We'll start in the red barn, where we keep the horses." I scurried up the porch steps and into the house. "Momma." I dropped my backpack in the foyer and darted into the kitchen. I could usually find my mom there if she wasn't at the farm store.

She was stirring a pot of what smelled like chili. Her brown hair was up off her neck and pulled into a neat bun, and her cell phone was plastered to her ear. "Thanks for telling me. Yes. I'll do that." Then she set her phone down on the counter beside the stove and placed the spoon on a dish next to her phone. "What's this I hear about you telling everyone at school that Tessa is pregnant? That's not you."

So much for keeping anything from Momma. "Who was that on the phone?"

Her eyebrows shot to her hairline. "What happened to your face?"

"It's nothing. A misunderstanding." *No lies.* She already knew anyway. I didn't have time to tell her what had happened since Sloane was waiting for me. "I need to show Sloane around, and I have chores. Can we talk later?"

She studied me for a moment. "Go. But this conversation isn't over."

I didn't think it was. "Oh, and Liam is working in the farm store." Then I hurried out of the kitchen through the sliding glass door and down the stone path that led to the horse barn.

Sloane stood outside with a stiff posture as though she were afraid to go in.

"Are you ready?" I asked.

She turned her head away from me, wiping her face.

"Are you crying? What's wrong?" Confusion made me tip my head to one side. Maybe she was afraid of horses like Maiken. But she'd told me she loved horses.

She puffed out a breath. "I'm fine."

No, she wasn't, but I couldn't force her to tell me.

Apple nickered, as did one of the other horses.

"The horses scent us," she said.

"Apple does for sure," I responded. "You want to go in?"

Suddenly, a dull pain clutched my chest as I felt her sorrow. She was hurting as she thought about or remembered something. I wondered if something had happened on her farm to cause her to cry.

She sighed. "In a minute."

"Are you sure you want to work here?" Maybe the farm wasn't the right place for her.

She swiveled her head toward me. Mascara smudged the underside of her eyes. "Yes. Now please stop the thousand questions." And just like that, her personality switched to the Sloane I was familiar with—cocky and snarky.

She was a paradox of sorts—sweet one minute, sad the next, and brazen the next.

I pivoted on my heel to cool the anger building inside me. My day was proving to be epic. First there was the rumor, then Momma was mad at me, and now Sloane's attitude. But all that washed away when I spotted Maiken jogging down the path.

I let out a low squeal, my heart fluttering.

Sloane turned around. "Great. My day just got worse."

I ignored her comment because my day went from bad to great.

"I should go," she said at the same time Maiken slowed to a swagger.

"What? You're on the clock," I said.

"I think you're right. I probably don't want to work here."

She started to leave, but I caught her arm. "You accepted the job. My dad won't give you a second chance."

Maiken, who was dressed in his running gear, settled his stance, wiping sweat from his brow with the sleeve of his T-shirt. "Are you working here now?" His blue eyes were glued to Sloane.

"Do you have a problem with that?" Her cranky personality went up several notches.

"I didn't see you in physics today. Don't think I'm going to help you catch up."

My mind raced. She left at lunch for a doctor's appointment, but physics was way before lunch. Maybe she got the time wrong, or maybe she was in the bathroom writing "Tessa Stevens is pregnant" when she should've been in physics. Although she could've done it during her free period that morning too.

She threw Maiken the finger. "I'm out of here."

He smirked.

I didn't. My dad was going to be furious.

She started for the path.

"Sloane," I said. "You won't be allowed back."

She took another step then another.

"Sloane," Maiken called out. "Stay away from my brother."

That stiff spine she'd had earlier turned to granite as she stopped in her tracks. Ever so slowly, she spun around, stomped back to Maiken, and poked him in the chest. "You don't get to tell me what to do." She swung her gaze to me. "And don't ever threaten me again." She marched away with her hands fisted at her sides.

I scratched my head, wondering how I'd threatened her. I'd only stated a fact. My dad wouldn't give her a second chance.

I couldn't help the next words out of my mouth. "Don't ever come back here," I called after her.

She raised her arm in the air and stuck up her middle finger then kept walking at a fast pace up to the lot of the farm store.

When I blinked, I saw my mom watching us from the kitchen. I expected her to call me in. Instead, she walked away. Well, I added another lengthy conversation with my mom to my list.

"She asked Marcus to homecoming," Maiken said through clenched teeth. "I shouldn't be so upset, but after her party, I don't think she's good for Marcus."

Sloane had some demons in her closet, especially given that she'd spent time in a mental health facility, but it wasn't up to Maiken who Marcus dated. "Maybe. But let Marcus decide. Remember my brother Carter didn't like you at first."

He sighed. "I know you're right. But I worry about my brother. I got to go. Kade has called a family meeting."

"Is it because of what happened at school today?"

Worry flashed across his face before he banked it. "I'm sure it is." He kissed me quickly on the lips. "Call you later?"

All I could do was nod.

With my head spinning, I headed into the barn. I had whiplash from Sloane and everything else that had transpired that day. But the day wasn't over yet.

Chapter 13

Maiken

I blew out breath after breath as I slowed to a jog down the driveway. My run had been invigorating yet irritating. Sloane had been the last person I'd wanted to see at the Thompson farm. But Quinn was right. Her brother Carter hadn't cared for me. He'd been overprotective of Quinn. He'd even told me to stay away from Quinn.

I wiped the sweat off my face. I was turning into Carter Thompson. Part of me knew I would be like him at some point, but I thought it would be from watching out for my sisters when boys dared to steal their hearts, not Marcus or any of my brothers.

But it wasn't his heart I was worried about. It was the fights, the split lips, the bloody eyes, and the drinking. All that could lead to something far worse, like he could end up in the hospital or… Yeah, I wasn't going there. I would go mad if I lost my brother.

I tore off my shirt as I scaled the porch and walked into an eerily quiet house. When I'd left, Marcus, Ethan, and Emma had been home. But I didn't hear the TV or any music that had filled the house earlier.

"Hello," I called out.

I checked the kitchen then the media room, which were connected by a ten-foot wide archway. They were both empty. I knew Lacey wasn't home. She'd been gone for close to a month for baseball road games.

Kade wasn't there either. He'd texted me that he was at the club

and to make sure everyone was home by five p.m. for our family meeting. I had a feeling he was going to lay down the law even harder than
he already had.

His rules were simple—stay out of trouble, study hard, be home by
curfew, and clean up after ourselves. All that was a piece of cake,
except Marcus hadn't stayed out of trouble, and now I had broken one
of Kade's rules too.

Nevertheless, part of me was ready for him to tell all of us that we
couldn't live with him and Lacey anymore.

The microwave blinked 4:45.

Using my T-shirt, I toweled the sweat off my arms and chest,
listening intently for any sound as I walked past the basement door, or
the first floor as Kade referred to the spacious part of the house. The
light was on downstairs, and a faint *thump* of bass trickled into my
ears.

When Kade and Lacey had the house built, they'd installed sound-
proof walls in the weight room to cut down on the noise. According to
Kade, the weight room could eventually become a music room one day
when they had kids.

I wandered downstairs and circled around to my right, trampling
through the game room, which had a pool table and a card table, much
like the boathouse. I passed a couch and two oversized chairs as I took
another right behind the stairs. The door to the weight room was
cracked open, and a bright light sprayed out.

The closer I got, the louder the *thump, thump, thump* of the music
became.

Pushing in the door, I found Ethan lifting weights. I crossed the
room and turned down the music on the stereo in the back corner.

He whipped his sweaty head around, startled, until he locked eyes
with me. "Don't freak me out like that."

"Where are Emma and Marcus?" I hadn't checked their bedrooms,
but I had a feeling they weren't there. Unless they had their head-
phones on, which they did on many occasions.

"Emma went over to see Aunt Eleanor, and Marcus said he was going out."

My voice went up a notch. "Kade will be home in fifteen minutes."

Ethan set down the weights and grabbed a towel from in between his legs. "You need to take a chill pill."

I wished I could, but the responsibility was on me to gather everyone for the meeting. So I got my phone out of a side pocket on my running pants and sent a group text to Emma and Marcus to get home.

After I hit the send button, I dropped onto the weight bench next to Ethan. "I've been wound so tight, I think I might explode."

He slapped a hand on my back. "Bro, you're carrying the weight of the world on your shoulders. I get it. You care. Sometimes too much. My advice—do something wild and crazy for once, like with your girl." He waggled his eyebrows. "Get my drift?"

I chuckled. "The more I make out with Quinn, the more I want to go all the way. And we're not ready for that."

He rolled his eyes. "Who said you have to have intercourse? There are other ways to have fun."

I envisioned all kinds of things between Quinn and me. "You're a year younger than me and seem so much older."

"I got a head start on you with girls," he said rather proudly. "Anyway, let's go upstairs. I've got to be in the locker room by six thirty. So Kade better make it quick."

I'd forgotten that Ethan had a football game that night. I should've asked Quinn if she wanted to go.

It's not too late, man. Call her. I would after our meeting if Kade didn't ground me for the fight at school.

Ethan swiped the towel over his face as we walked out. "Did Marcus tell you he was going to homecoming with Sloane?"

"I overheard him telling you as I was leaving for my run." *It's just a dance, nothing more.* The problem was I couldn't get Sloane's party out of my head or how drunk Marcus had been.

Ethan flicked off the light as we climbed the stairs. "She's not good for him."

I didn't say a word as we ambled into the kitchen. I grabbed two bottles of water from the fridge and tossed one to Ethan. When I unscrewed the cap, the front door opened then slammed shut so hard, the walls shook.

"Maiken!" Marcus shouted. "Where the fuck are you?"

Ethan and I froze.

I barely had time to set my water bottle down on the counter before Marcus lunged at me like a linebacker on the football team. Luckily, I managed to grab hold of the island. But my hand slipped, causing me to stumble and take Marcus with me. We hit the glass door so hard, the wind was knocked out of me.

Ethan pulled at Marcus, who fought him off.

"Who the fuck are you to tell Sloane to stay away from me?" Marcus shouted, his face beet red.

"She's all wrong for you," I said as calmly as I could.

He dove for me again. That time, I shook my head at Ethan. If Marcus wanted to get his aggression out on me, I would let him.

Marcus punched me in the gut, grunting as he kept doing it, pinning me against the glass doors until Kade ran in.

"What's going on?" Kade's voice dropped several octaves as he peeled Marcus off me.

Marcus snarled. "I don't tell you who you can date. And if you want to know my opinion, Quinn is not the girl for you. She makes you weak."

I doubled over, holding my stomach, breathing away the pain.

Kade pushed Marcus toward the media room. "Find a seat and sit your ass down."

"No," he said to Kade. "You're not my father, and I'm tired of you telling me what to do."

Hot rage washed over Kade. "Ethan, help Marcus into the media room. Maiken, get your ass in there too."

Ethan all but dragged Marcus into the room, and both sat on the L-shaped couch. I inhaled deeply, picked up my T-shirt, which had fallen out of my running pants, and eased down into one of two cushioned chairs adjacent to the couch.

"Next time I see Quinn, I'll be sure to tell her to stay away from you," Marcus said through clenched teeth.

Kade pierced me with a hard look, daring me not to respond as he marched into the media room, shoving his hand through his hair.

I had no idea how Marcus and I had gone from talking about hockey at lunch, to getting sent to the principal's office, to him wanting to put my head through a glass door.

Kade paced in front of the fireplace, his nostrils flaring like a fish trying to breathe out of water. "I went against my old man's wishes to not send you kids back to Georgia. I even coaxed Ms. Sanders to go light on you, but now I'm changing my mind. I get that none of you are in a good place. I get that you're still hurting for your dad." He glared at Marcus. "I even understand the drinking at the party." He eyed all of us. "What I will not put up with is all this fighting in my house. I will not tolerate disrespect for me, my wife, or the hatred I see in your eyes when you look at each other."

Ethan raised his hands. "Kade, we've never disrespected Lacey or you."

"That's where you're wrong," Kade said. "Lacey and I have opened our home and our lives for you. And the fact that you throw away family values like it's a piece of trash, like your brother is a piece of trash, shows great disrespect for what it means to be family. You should have each other's backs no matter if you agree or disagree with each other. No matter if your brother does something that you hate. No matter if your brother dates a girl you don't like. You're teenagers for Christ's sake. You're going to experience shit that adults won't like. But that's part of growing up. I'm not ancient, and it wasn't that long ago that I was in your shoes." He took a breath, and silence fell over us like a heavy veil.

Marcus crossed his arms and leaned back. Ethan pressed his elbows into his thighs, and I bounced my foot, my knee going up and down.

Kade stopped pacing. "Marcus, what is it going to take for you to stop acting like the world is out to get you?"

He let out an evil laugh. "I want my family to be a family again."

My heart split in two. "I'm sorry, Marcus. I shouldn't have told Sloane to stay away from you. Kade's right. I should have your back. But you need to make better decisions. You can't keep getting into fights and getting drunk."

"He's right, bro," Ethan said. "We love you. We don't want to see you get hurt."

A phone rang. It took me a second to realize it was Kade's.

Kade pressed the phone to his ear. "Hi, Christine. Everyone is here but Emma."

I wondered if he'd told Mom about all the crap that had been going on. If he had, then we would be moving to Georgia.

Kade tapped on the screen of his phone and set it on the coffee table. "Christine, you're on speaker."

All three of us said hi. I was about to add that Emma was at Aunt Eleanor's when the house door opened and shut.

Emma hurried in. "Sorry I'm late." Her brown gaze scanned the room. "What did I miss?"

"Your mom is on the phone," Kade said.

Emma took a seat on the other side of Marcus. "Hi, Mom."

"I hear everyone is doing great." Mom sounded nasally.

If she could see through the phone, she would see that each of us had our faces twisted. Kade hadn't ratted on us. Uncle Martin hadn't either.

Mom cleared her throat. "There's no easy way to say this, but Aunt Denise passed away early this morning."

We knew we would get this phone call at some point. Yet it didn't make the news any easier or less painful.

Marcus tore out of the room. Emma started crying. Ethan and I didn't react.

"Are you kids okay?" Mom asked. "Please tell me you are."

"We're worried about you," I said.

She didn't need to know that Marcus ran out or that Emma was quietly shedding tears.

"I'm heartbroken, but Aunt Denise is in a better place now." Mom sniffled. "I've got to make arrangements for her funeral. I would like all of you down here for that. You'll only miss a couple of days of school or three at most."

When Kade spoke, his tone was compassionate. "Once you have a date, let me know, and we'll head down."

Another funeral. Another death in the family.

As tears began to cloud my eyes, I prayed for our future, for our family, and hoped beyond hope that we didn't have another death in our family anytime soon.

Chapter 14

Quinn

I was looking out over the farm from my usual spot in the barn's loft, taking in the fall night air and thinking. My body was tired from all the chores I'd done, but my mind was working overtime on who had written those words on the bathroom mirror. A large part of me believed it was Sloane, mainly because she'd told Maiken she'd heard that Tessa was pregnant. That rumor hadn't gone around school. If it had, everyone would've heard that way before a message showed up on the mirror.

But there was no reason she should pit me against Tessa. How would she even know we'd been enemies? Whoever had written on the mirror had done it that morning before lunch. According to Sloane, she'd left school at lunch, but Maiken had said she hadn't been in physics that morning.

Something wasn't adding up.

"Sweet girl," Daddy called from down below before his heavy footfalls grew louder. Then he took a seat next to me, groaning as he did. "I'm getting old." He chuckled.

I scooted over a little. It was odd to see Daddy sitting in the loft with his legs dangling over the side.

"I used to do this all the time when I was a kid," he said. "I loved sitting up in the barn my parents had. So, your mom tells me Sloane didn't work. She left in a hurry?"

"I don't think this is the right place for her. I found her crying. I don't know why."

"Well, I hired her as a courtesy to her mom. She told me the hard work would be good for her daughter and that Sloane loves horses. But I need someone who's responsible."

"Don't get mad, but I overheard you telling Mom that Sloane had been in a mental health facility."

Giving me a sidelong glance, Daddy's stubbled jaw hardened. "That is not public knowledge, young lady."

"Do you know why?" I dared not tell him I'd already mentioned it to Maiken.

"That is not your business or mine. I expect you to keep that to yourself."

I got the impression he didn't know either. "Yes, sir. So she wasn't in juvie, then?"

"Not according to her mom."

Liam walked out of the barn, craning his neck up at me. "Quinn, are you sure you don't want to go to the football game?"

Celia had been texting me, trying to get me to go to the game with her and Liam. "Yeah." I didn't want to be the third wheel. I was actually tired from working my butt off anyway.

Daddy stood, albeit a little slowly, as he groaned. "Close up before you leave. I'm going up to the house."

"I'm sure Maiken is going," Liam said.

I hadn't heard from him since he'd left earlier. "He has that family meeting."

"But Ethan is playing," Liam fired back. "He always goes to watch his brother."

That was true. "I'll text him in a minute. You go. Maybe I'll see you and Celia there."

Once Daddy was outside, he said to Liam, "Don't stay out too late." Then he headed up the stone path, stopping to talk to Maiken, who was coming out of the house.

I hadn't heard or seen a car pull in. Then again, he might've jogged over like he had earlier.

I stabbed a finger at the house. "Maiken is behind you."

Liam spun on his heel and met Maiken halfway. They exchanged a bro hug and then words I couldn't hear. Liam gestured to me with his finger before continuing up to the house.

Butterflies began to take flight the closer Maiken got. When he reached the barn and looked up, those butterflies went wild. "I'm coming up."

"I'll come down." All of a sudden, I wasn't that tired. Maybe we could go to the game after all. If so, then I needed to take a quick shower.

I scrambled to my feet and brushed off the hay that was stuck to my hair and shirt, trying to look a little presentable. But it was no use. My body odor alone would scare him off. Sure, he'd seen me dirty and stinky before, but I didn't feel girly hugging my boyfriend while smelling like I'd swum in manure.

I was pulling straw off me when Maiken rounded the railing at the top of the stairs.

My hands froze on my shirt, and not because he looked handsome with his hair slicked back as though he'd just gotten out of the shower. Or because his soapy and manly scent drifted up my nostrils. Or because his jeans were slung low on his hips. "What's wrong?" The whites around his blue irises were red as though he'd been crying.

He didn't move, only stared at me as though debating what to do or say.

"Was the family meeting that bad?" Kade must've laid down the law so strictly that maybe Maiken couldn't see me anymore.

He shoved his hands into his jeans pockets, blinking as though he were trying not to cry.

Something more dire than punishment had happened.

"My aunt Denise died this morning. I knew this would eventually happen, but it still hurts like hell."

I covered my mouth with my hand.

A tear slid down his cheek.

A pain so sharp and deep clutched my chest. I ran to him, not caring if I smelled like Apple. His arms went around my waist while mine locked behind his neck.

"I'm so sorry," I whispered.

He hugged me tightly, sniffling. I couldn't help but cry with him. When he hurt, I hurt, and boy, was it a pain that took my breath away. He continued to sniffle as tears streamed down my face. I nudged my nose into his sweatshirt, which smelled like heaven.

Before I knew what was happening, he was lifting me up. Then we were moving until he set me down on a stack of hay high enough so that we were eye level.

He combed his fingers through my hair, searching my face through bloodshot eyes. "I couldn't wait to wrap my arms around you, to see your pretty face. I knew once I did, I would be okay." He continued to drag his hands through my hair, down my face, then back through my hair, his brain working overtime on something.

"Are you now?"

A weak grin emerged through his tears. Then his lips were on mine, hot, urgent, and desperate.

The boy did things to me that I was too shy to even admit. It scared me out of my mind that I was even thinking about more than kissing him. And it scared me out of my mind that my body was taking control and my brain was mush.

I knew there would come a time when Maiken and I would have sex. Maybe this was our time.

His hands, warm and rough, slipped under my shirt then around my waist to my lower back, rubbing a path up and down.

Goose bumps popped up all over. I let out a moan that sounded more like a whimper.

"Quinn." His voice was raspy yet painful. "I know this isn't the time, but I'm ready to take our relationship to the next level whenever you are."

All my muscles tensed. Over the summer, we'd talked about sex, and at that time, we'd agreed that neither of us were ready to consummate our relationship, although he'd told me it was getting tougher and tougher to abstain.

He pulled away, pain and sadness hanging over him like a dark cloud on a rainy day. "I'm sorry. I know you're not ready."

I couldn't help but recall the conversation Momma and I had had last year. Her advice was etched in my mind.

"First loves are extremely emotional, and those emotions can drive two people to make rash decisions without thinking. I want you to keep that in mind."

As much as I thought I might be ready, Maiken was in a very emotional state at the moment, and doing anything other than consoling him or kissing him wasn't appropriate.

He studied me. "Say something."

I clutched his sweatshirt. "Don't be sorry. But now is not the time."

He angled his head. "Are you saying you're ready, though?"

There was no one else on the planet I would give my innocence to. "I am, and I'm not."

He pressed his forehead to mine. "I'll wait for you forever, you know."

I shuddered, feeling warm and tingly all over.

We stayed tethered together, our chests rising and falling as though our hearts were beating as one.

I swallowed, the sound breaking the silence. "Did you know that when we look into each other's eyes for three minutes, our heart rates sync or beat together?"

He grinned. "Did you know that I give you my heart?"

It was my turn to kiss the lights out of him. I loved this boy so darn much that I was ready to give him more than my heart.

Chapter 15

Maiken

Three weeks had passed since Aunt Denise died, and during that time, life had been on autopilot. Everything had been one big blur.

Standing in front of the mirror in the Jack-and-Jill bathroom, I slipped on my suit jacket. I couldn't believe I was wearing a suit again. Twice within three weeks was epic for me. I'd worn the same black suit to Aunt Denise's funeral six days ago, and that night I was taking my girl to homecoming.

I couldn't wait to see her all dressed up. I couldn't wait to hold her in my arms. We hadn't spent a lot of time together since that night in her barn when I'd wanted her so darn badly, it had been hard to keep my hands where they belonged. She'd been right. That night had not been the right time to have sex. I'd been too emotional, and I wanted to make darn sure my head was clear and our first time was special.

Despite that, the last few weeks had been jam-packed with school, basketball practice, and Aunt Denise's funeral. Quinn had her own busy schedule, especially with putting in more work on the farm since her dad was down a person. He hadn't hired anyone yet to fill the hole Carter had left when he'd gone off to college.

The door from Ethan and Marcus's room slid open, and Marcus strutted in.

His blue gaze searched mine. "Why are you breathing heavy?"

He and I had been distant since that night when he'd rammed his fists into me in the kitchen. We'd hardly spoken even though I had apologized to him. I knew all of us were processing Aunt Denise's death. I knew he needed time as well.

"No reason," I said. He didn't need to know I was thinking of Quinn.

He'd threatened to tell Quinn to stay away from me, but he hadn't that I knew of. If he had, Quinn would've said something to me.

Kade had counseled me to give Marcus some space, and I had. But the less we talked, the more I felt like the tension between us was growing deeper and deeper.

Marcus was seeing Sloane steadily. Maybe Sloane was good for him because Marcus hadn't been in any fights.

"Are you excited about the dance?" I asked, praying he would open up to me.

His lips thinned. "Don't get in my business tonight."

I raised my hands midway. "Then don't give me a reason to." My tone was calm with no inflection of emotion.

His nostrils flared as he adjusted his red tie.

The theme of the homecoming dance was fire and ice, so the attire requirement was red, black, and white. We were both wearing red ties, white shirts, and black suits. I had no idea what Quinn was wearing except for the color scheme.

Ethan waltzed in, dressed the same sans the tie. "Everything okay in here?"

I glanced through the mirror at Marcus. His blue eyes were riveted to himself as he combed his hair back off his head.

I shrugged at Ethan, afraid to say anything that would set Marcus off. I didn't want to get into a fight or argument, so I went to my room. The idea of staying home barreled through me. My mood sucked.

Loosening my tie, I sat on my bed. My patience was wearing thin, and my heart was crumbling to ash. I had no idea how to fix things between Marcus and me. I was giving him space. But how much time did he need?

If Dad were alive, he would put an end to the animosity—somehow or someway. Mom would, too, but she hadn't noticed that Marcus and I weren't speaking. She hadn't noticed much. I couldn't blame her. After all, her sister had died, and the last thing I wanted to do was burden her with the problems between Marcus and me.

Bracing my elbows on my knees, I covered my face with my hands and said a prayer for my family, especially Marcus.

I loved living in Ashford. I loved living with Kade and Lacey. I liked that my aunt and uncle were only a quick jaunt around the lake. I loved that I had a girlfriend, friends at school, and basketball. But it was time for my siblings and I to live under one roof with Mom at the helm, and I was certain that would happen at some point now that Mom had buried her sister.

I straightened and unbuttoned my shirt, when Ethan came in.

"Are you not going to the dance?"

I would prefer to stay home and work out my aggression in the weight room. But I couldn't and wouldn't disappoint Quinn. "The tie is too claustrophobic."

He sat down beside me. "Marcus will be fine."

I snorted. "He hates me."

"He doesn't, bro. Aunt Denise just died. Give him time."

Silence hung in the air for a beat.

"Quinn will perk you up," he said.

I grinned, thinking about her. She did have a way of doing just that. So I buttoned my shirt as I stood. "Let's go have a good time."

He chuckled. "Maybe I can find a date while I'm there."

Some of the tension vanished as I started to fix my tie.

Kade poked his head in, appearing as though he hadn't slept in days. "You boys be safe tonight. Where's Marcus?"

"He left," Ethan said. "We should go. We're already late."

I eyed my watch. He was right. I was meeting Quinn like twenty minutes ago. I searched for my phone.

"Have fun. Any trouble, call me." Kade gave me the impression that trouble was right around the corner.

Ethan smoothed a hand over his head, taming his wavy crop of hair. "Are you expecting some?"

Kade chewed on the inside of his cheek, seemingly holding in a smirk. "You're teenagers. Right?"

He had a point. "Maxwells never get into trouble," I teased, but then a feeling of dread passed over me.

Brushing it off, I grabbed my keys, pocketed my phone, and headed out with Ethan. I would deal with whatever was in store that night. Besides, dancing with my girl couldn't get us into any trouble.

Chapter 16

Quinn

I waited for Maiken in the hall outside the gym, not far from the girls' restroom. I was also waiting for Celia. She'd gone in when we arrived about five minutes ago while Liam went to get us a table.

Kids dressed in their party best walked by, giggling and talking a mile a minute. The boys with their dates either had their shoulders hunched over or were fidgeting with their ties or shirts. It was evident they were uncomfortable.

I hoped Maiken could relax. He'd been through another death, and his mood had been quiet and somber, although we'd hardly seen each other. With more to do at the farm, I'd hardly had any free time in between studying and working. I also hadn't found out who had written the rumor about Tessa. Celia hadn't had any luck, and neither had Tessa. Aside from some girls asking Tessa if she were pregnant, the rumor didn't have much steam. I was chalking that incident up to a one-time thing.

I still believed Sloane was the guilty party, but she hadn't given any more indication or clues that it was her. In fact, she'd been in and out of school, or at least I hadn't seen her. Maiken told me that Marcus had been spending a lot of time with Sloane. I suspected she needed a friend.

I hadn't forgotten what Daddy and I had talked about, and other than Maiken, I hadn't said a word to anyone else about her time in a mental health facility.

Celia came out of the bathroom. Her dark hair was up in a twist like mine. We'd had our hair done at a local salon in town. Momma had given me some money to splurge on myself. I'd paid for the two-piece outfit I was wearing. I'd found a long-sleeved crop top in printed black lace, and I'd snagged a red skirt on the clearance rack at the dress shop in Ashford.

Celia patted her lips gently with her forefinger. "How's my lipstick?"

I giggled. "Burgundy is your color." I knew she was a nervous wreck. She and Liam had only been out once to the high school football game a few weeks back. That had been the night Maiken told me his aunt died.

Celia smoothed a hand down her white dress. It fell to her knees and was cinched at the waist, showing off her curvy figure. She looked great in white with her dark hair and dark eyes.

"Do you have your phone?" In my haste and excitement to leave, I'd forgotten my phone on my bed. I hadn't realized it until we'd arrived. Liam had offered to go home and get it, but I didn't think I would need it since I would be with Maiken.

"He's only fifteen minutes late," she said.

When Maiken and I had talked about homecoming, we'd decided that we would meet each other at the dance only because he had to drive Ethan and Emma. I'd asked about Marcus, and Sloane was picking him up.

Heels clicked along the floor, drawing my attention toward the entrance.

"Wow," Celia said. "Don't they look like the power couple?"

Tessa Stevens and Dustin Lane looked like they belonged on the cover of some Hollywood magazine. At that moment, I was envious of Tessa. She walked arm in arm with Dustin as though she were the star of an A-list movie, walking the red carpet. Her black hair was up and off her bare shoulders with thin strands curling around her face. Her red strapless ankle-length dress screamed "look at me."

"Who wears a tux to homecoming?" I asked Celia in a low voice. Dustin was dressed as if he were getting married. He filled out the black tux, white shirt, and red bow tie as though the suit was made for his broad shoulders. What had me blinking a few times was his gray eyes and how they stood out from his tux and black hair.

Dustin whispered something in Tessa's ear, and she let out a shy laugh.

When they approached, Tessa regarded Celia and me. "I love your dresses, ladies." Her tone was overly sweet. She wasn't the Tessa I knew who'd bullied me for many years, but I wasn't about to complain.

"Where's Maiken?" Dustin asked. "I want to talk to him about his brother Marcus. He's trying out for the hockey team."

I vaguely remembered Maiken mentioning that. "He'll be here."

"Is that why you're out in the hall?" Tessa asked.

I nodded. I would go in and sit at the table with Liam and Celia, but honestly, I couldn't sit. Besides, I wanted to walk in with Maiken, much like Tessa and Dustin.

"See you inside, then," Tessa said as the couple strolled away.

Once they were out of earshot, Celia squealed. "He is one handsome guy."

I playfully slapped her on the arm. "Hey, my brother is just as handsome."

"I know. I'm just making an observation. Besides, Dustin isn't my type. I like brown-haired boys."

I giggled. "Sure you do." Then I huffed. "Where is Maiken?" I was getting a little nervous. "Can I borrow your phone?"

She opened her wallet-style handbag and handed me her phone. No sooner had I pressed the home button than the main doors opened, and in walked Marcus and Sloane. I hesitated. Marcus would know where his brother was.

Unlike the power couple of Tessa and Dustin, Marcus and Sloane were far from giving me the sense that they belonged together. Maybe because Sloane was holding on to Marcus's arm for dear life. Her posture was stiff as a board, which I found odd since she usually came off as cool, badass, and relaxed. Maybe her tight black dress was squeezing all the air out of her. Everything on her stood out—her white-blond hair, her snow-white legs and arms, and her big breasts.

"Marcus looks so much like Maiken. Doesn't he?" Celia asked.

The brothers had blue eyes, but Marcus's hair was a shade darker, and his nose was slightly bigger.

More people came in behind Sloane and Marcus, but not one was Maiken.

Marcus and Sloane walked past, not saying a word to either Celia or me.

I ran up to Marcus. "Do you know where Maiken is?"

Sloane regarded me with her normal cocky attitude, pursing her bright-red lips. I swore her claws would come out at any second.

Marcus laughed, his alcohol-infused breath spraying down on me.

I took a step backward. "Have you been drinking?"

A cruel smile curled his lips. "Mind your own business." He narrowed his glossy eyes at me. "Oh, and stay away from my brother. You're no good for him."

Celia gasped.

The hairs lifted on the back of my neck. I was standing in front of Marcus Maxwell, but I blinked anyway to make sure I wasn't seeing someone different.

Sloane had a satisfied grin as she ambled alongside her date. The girl had a way of making me clench my hands into fists, much like Tessa once had.

"Didn't you say he got drunk at Sloane's party?" Celia asked.

"Wasted," I muttered, holding my stomach, which was full of even more nerves and unease because Marcus had been drinking. If Maiken found out, he was going to go through the roof like he had at Sloane's party.

"Please let this night go well," I mumbled to myself. I wanted one night with Maiken where there was no drama. But my intuition was warning me otherwise.

"Go find Liam," I told Celia. "I'm going outside to wait for Maiken." I didn't give her a chance to protest before I hurried down to the entrance. My stomach was in knots, not only from the encounter with Marcus, but because I was afraid maybe Maiken wasn't coming after all. Maybe he'd tried to call and tell me he was staying home. Marcus had said to stay away from Maiken. Maybe he knew something I didn't.

As I approached the entrance, I debated whether to tell Maiken that Marcus had been drinking. If I did, our night would be over before it had even begun. But if I didn't and Marcus ended up cut and bloody again, I would feel terrible. But what could Maiken do? Marcus wasn't falling over drunk. Maybe he'd just had one drink. I should mind my own business.

The door swung open, and Emma breezed in before Ethan and Maiken. She wore a white dress that fell to just above her knee. It was simple and elegant with double straps and a square neckline. Her hair was loose around her shoulders with part of it gathered off her fore-head and secured with a shiny clip.

"Wow, girl. You look amazing." Her tone was low as she leaned down. "My brother will love that outfit."

Yeah, Emma was much taller than me. In fact, her height made her stick out among her peers.

I paid her a compliment on how nice she looked, trying not to ignore her even though I had to talk to Maiken.

"Is something wrong?" asked Ethan, who came in before Maiken.

Both brothers wore black suits, white shirts, and no ties. They looked casual but sharp. I'd always thought ties made a man come off as stuffy.

I shook my head. "Just waiting for Maiken."

Maiken was checking something on his phone as he entered, but once he saw me, his jaw dropped.

"We'll catch you inside, bro," Ethan called as he and Emma started for the gym.

As soon as Maiken grabbed my hand and tugged me out of the way of the kids coming in behind him, I lost all thought.

His gaze swept over me with hooded eyes and a grin that about knocked me out. "Holy Moley. You look incredible." Then his hand was on my stomach. "I like that you're showing a little skin here."

I knew he would like the crop top. It was rather revealing yet not so much as to dub me a hussy.

"I really don't think we should go in," he said, his voice strained.

I would agree. I would rather find somewhere quiet and just hang out, although I wanted to slow dance with him. I wanted to feel what it was like to have his arms around me while we swayed to a slow song sung by Kody.

At the last minute, the scheduled band had canceled due to an illness. Kody and his girlfriend, Jessie, had stepped up. Actually, rumor around school was that Sloane Price had suggested the committee ask the talented Maxwell.

"One dance," I said. "Then you can take me anywhere you would like."

His eyebrows shot to his hairline. "Careful. I might take you back to my bedroom."

Promise? My cheeks flushed. "We should find Celia and Liam."

He held out his elbow. "Your chariot awaits."

I hooked my arm through his just like Tessa had done with Dustin. As we walked arm in arm down the long hallway, euphoria overpowered my senses, and I felt like the luckiest girl at Kensington High.

Chapter 17
Maiken

As soon as I laid eyes on Quinn, everything else around me blurred. The only person I wanted to talk to, dance with, and kiss all night long was Quinn Thompson, who, by the way, had my suit pants growing tighter and tighter with every step we took toward the *thump, thump, thump* of the music.

My pulse was going crazy as I slyly checked her out.

Holy hell.

Her lavender-vanilla scent was making me lightheaded. If that weren't doing the trick, her long neck, her long legs—which seemed to go on forever in those three-inch heels—and her two-piece outfit revealing her tight stomach were sending me over the edge. My willpower to be a gentleman could very well break by the night's end.

Dude, take it down a notch.

An upbeat song pounded out of the speakers that flanked the stage, bursting my Quinn bubble as we entered the gym. It took me a second to take in the scene. I was used to walking onto a basketball court complete with bleachers and bright lighting. Instead, the bleachers were tucked up against the wall, creating floor space for the round tables that were scattered about. The lights above were dim, spraying down a soft glow. The effect created a dreamy mood that I was sure I could get lost in with Quinn in my arms.

"The homecoming committee did a nice job," Quinn said, scanning the room.

The fire-and-ice theme was rather cool. Flaming table torches served as centerpieces, people were drinking from flashing LED goblets, lighted cubes were stacked around, and glittery stuff hung from the ceiling. More glowing red and white decorations complimented the fire-and-ice theme. Not to mention, the attire for the theme was all kinds of cool. Some girls were dressed in all white, some in all red, and others had combinations of red and white or red and black like Quinn.

Liam came out of nowhere. "We're over here." He pointed to a table near the wall and away from the stage.

Quinn let go of me and headed for the table.

"Dude, where's your tie?" Liam asked. "Weren't we supposed to wear them?" He tugged on his red bow tie.

"I have a white shirt on," I teased. I spotted other guys with no ties as well. A couple of them weren't even wearing suit jackets.

"Well, I'm taking mine off." He proceeded do just that. "Dustin Lane is looking for you. He wants to talk to you about Marcus. I didn't know Marcus was trying out for hockey."

I nodded. "Have you seen Marcus?"

We ambled over to the table. Celia, Emma, and Quinn were huddled together, chatting, giggling, and pointing toward the dance floor.

"Marcus was at the refreshment table last I saw," Liam said.

I checked to see where the refreshments were set up across the room along the sidewall. I didn't see Marcus, but I did see Ethan talking to Dustin Lane.

Don't worry about Marcus. Have a good time.

The girls stopped talking when Liam and I approached.

Quinn patted the empty chair next to her, batting her lashes with one of her shy looks.

The song ended, and the singer cleared her throat. "How's everyone doing tonight?"

Whistles and cheers erupted as kids gathered closer to the stage.

The five of us shifted our attention to Jessie Ryan. Kody's girl-friend gripped the mic. The light around her highlighted the tattoos on her fingers. "Thanks for having us. I'm sorry the band you had scheduled to play couldn't make it, but I promise we'll keep you on the dance floor."

"We love you, Jessie," a boy in the crowd shouted from somewhere in the room.

Liam leaned into me and whispered, "She's hot as hell."

I couldn't argue with him. Jessie was pretty. She had a mane of streaks—blond, brown, and red—and green eyes that could mesmerize a person. Not me, though. The only girl who could suck me in was Quinn Thompson.

Jessie laughed. "I love you too." Then she glanced at Kody, who had a guitar strapped around his body, and she nodded at the drummer, Jake Trent. When she did, the girls squealed.

"We love you, too, Jake," a girl screamed.

"And Kody," another girl chimed in.

"I think we should take up music instead of basketball," Liam teased.

Quinn, Celia, and Emma were riveted to the stage.

"This next song is the one that started everything for us." Jessie took the mic off the stand and went over to Kody, who was eyeing her as though she was the moon, the stars, and the whole universe. "Kody wrote this song when he and I met." She locked eyes with him. "I think when I first heard him play this on the piano, I fell in love with him then." She lifted up on her toes and kissed him.

A collective sigh zinged around the room as a few couples got closer to each other.

I couldn't help but do the same. Closing the distance between Quinn and me, I leaned down and put my lips to her ear. "You're the only girl in the room for me."

She shivered.

"Gather your dates and get close," Jessie said.

Kody strummed his guitar as Jessie started singing.

I've drifted through the days, thinking of you. I've wandered through the fields, wondering what could've been. You were the one who touched my soul. You gave me love. A chance to feel again. Come play with me. Tease me. Tempt me. Dare me to live again.

"Would you like to dance?" I asked in Quinn's ear.

She didn't hesitate.

We joined the others who were moving their feet, their bodies pressed together as Jessie lulled us into a romantic state.

Quinn locked her hands around my neck while mine went around her waist. As soon as my hands touched her warm, soft skin, an electrical charge connected us as she pressed her body into mine.

"It seems the Maxwells have a way with words," she teased, craning her neck up at me. "Kody writes songs, and you write poems."

I was nothing like my cousin. The man had a knack for songwriting. My poems were cheesy at best.

More couples came onto the dance floor, making it impossible for anyone to move. I didn't mind since I didn't know what I was doing anyway. I rested my head against Quinn's, but then someone fell into me.

I clutched Quinn tightly so she wouldn't fall into the couple next to us. Once I got my bearings, I turned to tell the person that bumped me to watch where they were going. But when I did, my stomach tightened at the sight of Marcus and Sloane, and not because they were dancing together, but because he seemed off.

Marcus laughed then threw me the finger.

I let go of Quinn and gave Marcus my full attention. "Have you been drinking?" It was a stupid question because I could smell the liquor on him.

"He has," Quinn said.

My jaw flexed. "You knew he was drinking?"

She shook her head. "I smelled it on him when he came in."

Marcus swatted his hand at me. "Chill, bro. You really don't want to make a scene. Do you?"

I clutched Marcus's arm hard, not caring who was watching or taking pictures.

The music played on, but the couples around us stopped dancing.

Breathe, man. Give him space. Let him do his thing. He needs time.

So I let go of Marcus. I came to the dance to have fun with Quinn. I came in hopes I wouldn't have to worry about Marcus or anyone.

Marcus pushed people out of the way, stumbling in the process, and that sent a jolt of worry through me. He could get suspended if he got out of hand.

Sloane started to chase him, but I blocked her. "This is the second time you've gotten him drunk. Have you been drinking too?"

She glared, pursing her lips.

My nostrils flared as I sniffed the air around her like I was a damn dog. I couldn't smell any alcohol, but that didn't mean anything.

She darted around me and took off.

I stood there, dizzy, unfocused, and enraged, so much so I swore I couldn't see straight.

The couples who'd stopped dancing started moving again.

Quinn touched my back. "We should make sure they don't leave. I mean, if they've been drinking."

Her words shook me from my zombie state as my brain and body kicked into gear. She had a point. I didn't want Sloane driving if she'd been drinking. So I hurried off the dance floor. Even if she hadn't been drinking, Marcus and I needed to hash shit out once and for all. Homecoming wasn't the place to do that, but Marcus was forcing my hand.

Ethan caught up to me. "What's going on?"

"We need to find Marcus. He's been drinking."

"Leave him alone, bro," Ethan said. "So he's had a drink."

"You knew too?"

He shrugged. "I smelled the liquor on him."

Unbelievable. Was I the only one who wanted to make sure no one else in my family died?

I let out a laugh that didn't sound like me at all. "So do you want our brother to get into a car with a girl that has been drinking too?"

His jaw came unhinged. "Sloane is drunk?"

"I don't know. But I'm not taking any chances." I left Ethan standing there while I went in search of Marcus.

I didn't care if my brothers hated me. I didn't care if they never spoke to me again. Sure, maybe I was being overly dramatic, but I didn't care.

The hall outside the gym was empty. I checked both the girls' and boys' bathrooms but found nothing.

Heels clicked on the floor behind me as I darted outside and into the parking lot. I barely registered the lights and the engine before Quinn shouted my name.

I turned in her direction for a second before the impact of the car against my spine threw me in the air. I heard brakes screech. Quinn screamed.

The wind gushed out of me, and breathing became a monumental task. I labored for breath after breath, but I couldn't get air into my lungs.

I was going to die.

I was going to join my dad in heaven.

The screams and voices dulled to a hum as I began to fade. I tried to lift my head, but it felt like someone was holding me down.

I had to get up. I had to find Marcus.

I heard more screams, more loud voices.

A hand waved over me. "Maiken." Quinn's voice sounded like an angel's. Then she was tapping on my face. "Someone call an ambulance. You're going to be okay."

Suddenly, the sky above me started spinning, and I couldn't hold my eyes open anymore.

Chapter 18

Quinn

Oh my God! Sloane Price is going to die if anything happens to Maiken. I can't believe she hit him.

I fell to my knees at Maiken's side, tapping his face as my tears poured. "Don't close your eyes." He needed to stay alert. He needed to stay awake.

I felt for a pulse then cried harder.

The sirens blared in the distance as a crowd formed.

Large, warm hands landed on my arms. "Quinn," Kody said in my ear. "Come with me."

I shook my head. "I'm not leaving him."

Jessie dropped to her knees on the other side of me, placing her fingers on Maiken's carotid artery. "Quinn, go with Kody. I got this."

"But I couldn't feel his pulse," I cried.

"The ambulance is on the way," she said. "Kody, call your brother. Have him meet me at the hospital." She got on her phone. "Yes, this is Nurse Ryan. We have a seventeen-year-old male that was hit by a car. Head injury and possible bodily injury. Yes. He has a weak pulse."

I'd forgotten that Jessie was a nurse before she made it big in the music industry. All I cared about at that moment, though, was her helping Maiken.

Kody guided me over to Emma, who was standing alone, crying and shivering. I hugged her hard, more for me than her. I needed someone to hold me. I needed someone to tell me Maiken was going to be okay.

Her arms came around me tightly. "I can't believe this."

I couldn't either. We cried together, and as the sirens grew louder, so did our sobs. I dared not look behind us. I dared not look at all the people watching. I dared not lay eyes on Sloane either.

"I swear. Sloane is dead if anything happens to Maiken," Emma said.

The urge to rip off Sloane's head was strong, but that wouldn't accomplish anything.

I pulled away from Emma to search the crowd for her and Marcus. All I could think about when they'd left the dance was Alex Baker. He'd died last year when a drunk driver hit him.

She stood next to her car, crying as Ethan held Marcus back from Maiken. Pain swam in Marcus's eyes as he fixated on Maiken.

Ethan said something to him in his ear.

Marcus shook his head as tears flowed down his face. Then he buried his head in Ethan's shoulder.

The ambulance pulled up. The paramedics didn't waste any time in getting their gear.

I let out a sigh, holding on to Emma. Both of us were tense.

Dead silence filled the night air except for the paramedics, who were talking to Jessie as they braced Maiken's neck, lifted him gently onto a stretcher, and got him into the ambulance.

Jessie kissed Kody then hopped into the ambulance.

I hurried over. "I want to go."

Jessie regarded me with sad green eyes. "You can meet us at the hospital." She shut the doors as the lady paramedic was busy hooking Maiken up to an IV.

The ambulance sped off, passing a cop car that drove up.

I stood in the middle of the aisle, not far from where Maiken had gotten hit. Time froze. I knew I should move out of the way of the police cruiser, but my legs wouldn't move.

"Quinn," Kody said softly. "Maiken is in good hands." He guided me out of the way of the cop car and back to Emma, who was staring at the ground. Then he marched over to Ethan, Marcus, and Sloane.

I didn't see Liam until he was hugging me. "Maiken will pull through."

I sobbed into his chest. "Y-you d-didn't see h-him get hit. Sloane hit him. Sloane hit him."

He rubbed my back. "Shhh. We'll go to the hospital."

"What happened?" a familiar deep baritone voice asked.

I eased away from my brother.

"Officer Daniels," Liam said.

Officer Daniels settled in front of us with a wide stance. "Quinn. Liam. Did you see what happened?"

Liam and I knew Officer Daniels well. He and Daddy had gone to high school together.

I wiped my nose with the back of my hand. "I did." I leaned against the same parked car as Emma.

Officer Daniels took in the crowd. Chaperones were guiding kids back into school. Kody, Ethan, Marcus, and Sloane were gathered in front of her car.

Another police cruiser pulled up.

"Tell me what happened," Officer Daniels said.

"Maiken was looking for his brother Marcus." I pointed at Marcus, who was watching us. "Anyway, Maiken ran out of the building, and that's when he got hit."

Officer Daniels stabbed a thumb at Sloane. "By that car?"

"Yes, sir," I said.

The other cop got out of his car, and Officer Daniels pivoted on his heel. "Wait here." He met his colleague halfway, and the two exchanged words that I couldn't hear.

I swallowed, praying they would arrest Sloane. If they didn't, I would do something drastic like lock her in our pigpen and throw away the key. She deserved to feel every bit of the pain that Maiken was feeling and that I was feeling.

"Quinn," Celia called from somewhere close by. "Liam?"

I searched the area as Principal Sanders shuffled Celia and others into the building.

"You should go," I said to Liam. "Be with Celia."

He unbuttoned the collar of his shirt. "Sis, I'm not leaving you."

The cops were still talking. I didn't understand why they weren't asking Sloane or Marcus questions.

I blinked once then twice. I had to do something. I couldn't wait around. "Take me to the hospital," I said to Liam. "I need to get out of here."

"Daniels probably won't let us leave," he said.

Emma finally came out of her frozen state. "I'm going too."

I stomped off, heading to Liam's truck, which was parked on the other side of the lot, behind Sloane's car.

"Quinn, don't go far," Officer Daniels said.

I didn't care if he tried to stop me. Besides, he knew where I lived. The closer I got to Sloane and Marcus, the more I seethed. I had so much rage, I was about to explode.

Emma and Liam were right on my heels.

Sloane straightened the closer I got. Marcus didn't move. Ethan didn't either. Kody, on the other hand, lowered his phone from his ear.

But before anyone had a chance to stop me, I punched Sloane right in the face. "I hope you feel that pain, which is nothing compared to what you did to Maiken."

Sloane brought her hand to her nose.

I wanted to wince from the pain ricocheting up my arm from hitting her. *Wow!* I'd never punched anyone before. I'd hoped I would feel better, but the physical pain I felt in my hand and arm did nothing to ease the emotional pain waging a war inside me.

The cops rushed over as Liam tugged me away.

I regarded Officer Daniels. "I'm going to the h-hospital." I didn't give him a chance to respond. I didn't want to hear Sloane and her excuses either.

All I wanted to do was see Maiken.

One of the police radios crackled as I stomped away. My heart seemed to crackle along with it.

If Liam weren't going to drive me, then I would walk. The hospital wasn't that far from school anyway. On second thought, I felt the urge to run. I took off my heels and dashed into the wooded area that separated the main school building from the sports complex.

"Quinn," Liam shouted. "Where are you going?"

"I need some time alone." Then I ran, not caring that sticks and dirt were poking the bottoms of my bare feet. I didn't register any pain except for the pain in my chest.

I was to blame for Maiken getting hit by Sloane. I shouldn't have called his name. I was the one who'd distracted him. I should've minded my own business and stayed inside while the brothers hashed out their differences.

I ran around the school to the front side then kept going across the empty parking lot until I was walking down a dimly lit side street.

Tears raged on.

I slowed to a walk, sniffling when an engine rumbled and headlights bounced toward me. Then Liam's truck came into view.

He braked, rolling down the passenger window. "Get in."

I hesitated, shuddering.

"Sis." His tone was gentle. "Maiken needs you."

I wasn't sure about that. I wasn't sure he would want to see me. I wasn't sure if our relationship would be the same after this. But I had to know he was all right. I had to tell him I was sorry.

Chapter 19

Maiken

"Maiken." A sweet and airy voice trickled into my psyche. "Maiken, you need to wake up."

Beeps and voices registered from somewhere around me. I took in a breath and groaned in excruciating pain. It felt like I'd been slammed into a wall over and over again.

I tried to move, but my neck, head, and chest hurt. Then I inhaled, and tears pricked my eyes. Pain. There was so much pain in my chest.

"Don't move," a deep voice said.

How could I move? It hurt too damn much.

A bright light flashed in my eyes.

"Vitals are normal," the female voice said.

My gaze darted from left to right, finding a tall man on one side of me and a pretty lady on the other.

"How is he?" I knew that voice.

"Jessie," I whispered, blinking several times.

Jessie appeared at the foot of my bed. Her green gaze was filled with worry. "Hey, big guy."

That light flashed in my eyes again. "I'm Dr. Navar, one of the emergency room doctors. Can you tell me your name?"

I tried to sit up and winced.

"Easy," Dr. Navar said. "Can you tell me your name?" he asked again.

I thought for a second, hoping my brain would fire on all cylinders, or at least one. "Maxwell." My voice didn't sound like me. "I mean, Maiken Maxwell."

"Good. Do you know what happened to you?"

I closed my eyes, searching my data bank. Images of Quinn and me slow dancing popped into my brain. A warm feeling blanketed me. Then in an instant, chills made me shiver as I ran to find Marcus.

My eyes shot open. "Marcus. Is Marcus okay?"

The machines in the room went haywire. I struggled for breath. Air. I needed air, just like I'd needed air when I was lying on the ground. "It hurts to breathe." I barely got the words out of my mouth.

"Roxanne, call down to imaging and see when they can get a CT and MRI done."

"Maiken," Dr. Navar said. "I'm going to press along your chest and abdomen, and I want you to tell me if anything hurts." He pressed all over my abs and chest. "Anything?"

"No."

He felt around my neck and gently moved my head to one side.

I groaned. "That hurts."

He moved my neck to the other side.

I groaned again as the room spun a little. "Pain."

"Do you feel any nausea?" he asked.

"Just dizzy now."

Removing a long, pointy metal device from his lab coat, Dr. Navar went to the bottom of the bed. "Maiken, I want you to tell me if you can feel anything."

Jessie lifted the blanket up for him.

Then Dr. Navar dragged the metal device over my right foot. "Do you feel that?"

I blinked rapidly. "No."

He tested my other foot as he locked eyes with me. I shook my head. He kept dragging that device over the tops of my feet then the bottoms again. I couldn't feel anything.

Fuck! What is happening?

I shook my head but shouldn't have. The pain in my neck was enough to make me cry.

"Can you wiggle your toes?" he asked.

With all the concentration I had, I tried to wiggle my toes, but they weren't moving. Reality was slowly clearing away the haze around my brain. In that moment, my pulse climbed higher and higher as I started to realize that while I could feel pain in my neck, chest, and head, I couldn't feel any sensations in my feet.

Lift your leg.

With each try, a tear escaped, one by one, breath by breath. Sweat beaded on my forehead. I wanted to feel something in my legs and feet, anything to indicate that I was still whole, still able to walk, still able to play basketball, and fuck, still able to dance with Quinn.

Dr. Navar pocketed his metal device. "Maiken, we're going to run some tests, and then we'll get a better picture of what's going on."

I wanted to ask his opinion of why I couldn't feel any sensations in my feet. But I was afraid to hear his answer. I was afraid that the moment he told me would be the moment I would curl up into a ball and shut myself off from the world.

"Do you remember getting hit by a car?" Dr. Navar asked.

I remembered Quinn calling me, and the next thing I remembered was the screech of brakes. Then my body was bouncing off the car and onto the ground. "Yeah."

He tipped his head toward the door. "Jessie, can I talk to you outside?"

The cuff around my arm squeezed and kept squeezing until it released. Then the machine next to my bed beeped. I would bet that my blood pressure was just as high as my heartbeat as I dug deep to remember more of what had happened. But Quinn, needing air, and the sound of brakes were the three things that came to mind other than running out of the building to find Marcus.

The room I was in had a glass wall that allowed me to see Dr. Navar's lips move as Jessie bobbed her head.

This is bad. Very, very bad.

The machines around me beeped out of control.

Jessie folded her arms over her chest as Dr. Navar walked away. She stood there, seemingly frozen, until something caught her attention. She started forward and held up her hands.

Marcus appeared. His hair was wild, his shirt was hanging out of his pants, and his face was red. "I want to see him."

She gripped his arms. "Not now."

He pushed past her, or maybe she gave in. He came to an abrupt halt when he saw me. His blue eyes were dark, red, and splotchy.

As hard as it was for me to breathe, I let out a huge sigh just the same. Aside from him crying and the big spot of what looked like puke on his shirt, he didn't look hurt. When he'd run out of the dance, I'd had a bad feeling that something would happen to him. Instead, that bad feeling had been about me.

Marcus shuffled up to my bedside, his blue gaze scraping up and down my body. I swore it felt like the edge of a blade dragging along my skin.

I tried to move my arm, but the effort was unbearable. Even breathing was hell.

He cried, his tears falling one by one onto my bare arm.

"I'm okay," I said lowly, choking back my own tears. I was far from okay, but I had to be strong for him, for me, and for my family. The problem was that I wasn't sure any amount of strength would help.

You shouldn't lie to him. I had nothing concrete to tell him. He didn't need to know I couldn't move my legs, at least not right now.

He flicked hair from his eyes with a trembling hand. "I'm sorry. I'm so, so sorry."

"For what? For getting drunk?" He wasn't old enough to drive. So he couldn't have been the one to hit me. "It's not like you put me in this hospital bed."

He broke out into a quiet sob, his shoulders shaking.

The machines sang rapidly, indicating how fast my pulse was

pounding. Since I'd come to only a few minutes ago, I hadn't had time to consider who'd hit me. But the way Marcus was sobbing… I couldn't even comprehend that he could've been driving.

Regardless, if he had been behind that wheel, he didn't need me yelling or angry. He didn't need to carry the weight of hitting his brother around with him. He was already in a bad place with the way our lives had changed since Dad had died. I didn't want him to take on any other bad shit.

Marcus shuddered a breath. "Sloane hit you."

Relief pushed its way down, and anger wormed its way up. I guess I shouldn't have been surprised. Sloane had been nothing but mayhem since we'd met her.

"Say something," Marcus whispered.

I had no words. What was I going to say? That I forgave her? How could I? I was in a freaking hospital bed in pain, and who knew what else was happening to me?

"Where's Ethan and Emma? Quinn?" I didn't want to talk about Sloane.

Marcus's face twisted. "That's all you have to say? You're not going to yell or tell me what to do?"

I inhaled a quiet breath, pushing through the pain that had a hold on my ribs. In that moment, I looked at my brother and saw a frightened little boy who had never been scared of much growing up. But the fear washing over him caused my heart to hurt as much as my chest.

"I love you. That's all I have to say."

He stared at his feet. "I wish I could go back in time."

Me too. "Was she drunk?" If I recalled, I hadn't smelled any liquor on her, but that didn't mean anything.

He raised his head. "She had a sip of my drink."

I clutched the blankets, my anger growing. "Did she not see me?"

He slipped his hands into his pants pockets. "No. She dropped her phone on the floor near her feet. So she bent down to pick it up and, at the same time, pressed on the gas instead of the brakes. When I screamed at her, she looked up but not in time. I'm sorry, Maiken."

Quinn had told me that Sloane had never been in juvie but in a mental health facility. As I listened to Marcus, I was curious if he knew.

"How much do you know about her?" I asked.

"She told me she spent some time in a mental health facility. Her dad died in a bad fire, and she had a rough time. She hurts like us, Maiken."

"I'm sorry she lost her dad, bro. But drinking or her giving you liquor to take away the pain isn't going to bring our dad or her dad back." I understood that everyone processed death differently, but I was hoping maybe Marcus would see that his behavior had been destructive.

Jessie knocked on the open door. "Marcus, it's time for you to head out to the waiting room. Your brother needs to have some tests done."

Marcus crossed his right arm over his chest to grip his left. "Is everything okay?"

"Just a checkup," I said.

He slowly backed away with so much regret, pain, and sadness in his blue eyes. "I'll let Ethan and Emma know you're good."

As soon as Marcus left, I sighed. "Tell me the truth, Jessie. Will I walk again?" As much as I didn't want to hear that I might not walk again, I had to know.

"Let's wait to see what the scans tell us," she said.

"Can I see Quinn?"

She frowned. "Not right now, big guy. The technician should be in shortly."

Quinn was probably freaking out. I knew I would be if she were in here. But maybe it was best I didn't see her right then. I would like to have good news to tell her and my family. Still, if the possibility existed that I would never walk again, I wasn't sure Quinn would want to be my girlfriend. I would never be able to chase her like I'd done many times in August down by the lake. We would never again be able to walk hand in hand like we did all the time. I would never be able to lift her up and into my arms or dance with her.

Jessie patted my arm. "Don't think the worst."

I swore she was in my head. Then again, she probably counseled patients all the time.

Regardless, no amount of counseling would help me come to terms with being paralyzed.

Chapter 20

Quinn

I was sitting in the waiting room, bouncing my knee and biting my nails. Only ten minutes prior, I'd been pacing. Ten minutes before that, I'd been in the bathroom—anything to keep my mind from thinking Maiken was on his deathbed.

The voices of the guys on the basketball team hummed nearby. All but two were there. Ethan and Emma were hanging by the doors that led into where the hub of the emergency room existed, waiting for Marcus to come out or maybe waiting to go in. He'd somehow gotten through the locked doors that read Hospital Personnel Only.

I had a mind to do the same if someone didn't tell us soon what was going on.

Chase, who had been talking to the team, sauntered over and sat in the empty chair that moments ago had been occupied by Liam, who'd found a quiet spot on the other side of the room to talk on the phone. I imagined he was talking to Celia. She hadn't been able to get past Principal Sanders after the cops arrived at school. Considering Liam was her ride, I would guess she was stuck at the dance for the moment.

Chase reached over and placed his hand, warm and rough, on my knee that was bouncing like a basketball. "He's going to get through this."

I laughed, albeit nervously. "We don't even know how he is. So how can he get through it?" My tone was equal parts harsh and panic.

Chase took off his suit jacket and draped it over my shoulders. He probably thought my trembling meant that I was cold. Maybe I was. But my body felt numb. I swore if someone stuck a pin in me, I wouldn't feel it.

"What's taking them so long?" I asked, shuddering.

The emergency room doors flew open, and Marcus came out. He sighed as his shoulders slumped, which signaled to me that he'd seen Maiken and his brother wasn't a pulse away from dying.

I should've been happy, but my tight muscles and the knot in my stomach wouldn't loosen until I heard Maiken's prognosis from a medical professional.

Marcus continued to talk while Emma and Ethan listened. According to Emma, after the police had questioned everyone, they'd taken Sloane down to the police station until they could get a hold of her parents. Marcus had been released into Kade's custody.

Speaking of Kade, he was on the phone, too, wearing a hole in the floor in front of the information desk. Worry and anger were written all over his face as he listened to the person on the other end.

Marcus hugged Ethan, or maybe Ethan hugged Marcus. I was ready to run over to them to get some answers, but Marcus glared at me. Or maybe his scowl was meant for Chase. I discarded the last thought unless Chase had done something to Marcus that I didn't know about.

"Marcus looks like he wants to punch one of us," Chase said in a low voice.

"It's me. I punched his girlfriend." I showed him my right hand.

He ran his fingers over the bruised knuckles. "Whoa! Way to go, Quinn. I knew you had some feistiness in you."

It wasn't anything but pure rage.

The doors that led to where Maiken was opened again, and Jessie walked out. Strands of her brownish hair fell loose from her bun-type hairstyle. She appeared distraught as she twirled a ring on one of her fingers. She corralled Ethan, Emma, and Marcus, and came over to all of us who were scattered around the room.

Liam pocketed his phone, as did Kade.

Once everyone was quiet, Jessie spoke. "Maiken is doing fine. He's alert, bruised, and in pain."

I bit my lip. Of course he was in pain after the car plowed into him. I didn't know how fast Sloane had been going, but she'd sped up for some reason, as if she'd seen Maiken and wanted to hit him.

"The doctor is with him. No one will be allowed to see him tonight. I suggest everyone go home. It's late anyway, and he needs to rest."

I wasn't leaving. I would sleep there if I had to.

"I want to see him," I blurted out.

Jessie gave me a sad smile. "I'm sorry, Quinn. If anyone sees him tonight, it will be family."

I wanted to protest but didn't want to sound like a five-year-old. Besides, maybe he didn't want to see me. After all, I was the one who'd distracted him. I was the reason he'd gotten hit by a car.

Jessie guided Kade down a hallway until they were out of sight.

The basketball team said their goodbyes and told Chase and Liam to call with updates.

Liam pulled out his keys. "Quinn, let's go. We'll come back tomorrow during visiting hours."

"I'm not leaving," I said.

"I can stay with her," Chase said.

Liam harrumphed. "No offense, dude, but you're not staying here alone with my sister all night."

"It's not up to you," I said to Liam. I didn't need Chase by my side, but if he wanted to keep me company, I wouldn't mind, although I wouldn't be good company.

"You're right," Liam said. "But Mom called and told us to get home."

Kade padded over without Jessie. "Kids, let's go. Maiken can't have any visitors right now. Jessie will keep us updated."

Ethan, Emma, and Marcus didn't argue. They filed out of the building, not saying anything to me. I found it odd that at least Emma didn't say goodbye.

Kade dangled his keys. "Quinn, I promise. I'll call you the minute he's allowed visitors."

"Why do I get the feeling you know something but aren't telling us?" I asked Kade.

He studied me with those piercing copper eyes that reminded me of my dad's when he was irritated. "Here's what I know." A muscle jumped along his strong jaw. "It's late, and Maiken needs rest. And if anyone is going to see him, it will be me."

"Marcus saw him." As soon as the words left my mouth in a whiny tone, I wanted to take them back. The last thing I wanted to do was make Kade mad.

"Get some rest, Quinn." Kade turned and left the emergency room.

Tears stung my eyes. I felt like Daddy had just reprimanded me.

Chase stood. "He's right. We need to get some sleep. I can pick you up tomorrow, Quinn, and we can sit in here all day and wait."

It was sweet of Chase to offer, but for some reason, I wasn't sure I wanted to come back. I was getting the feeling that Maiken's family didn't want me around. I knew I was being a brat, but that was how I felt.

Rising, I handed Chase his jacket. "Th-thank y-you." I was on the verge of sobbing.

He kissed me on the cheek. "I'll call you in the morning."

Then only Liam and I were left.

My brother wrapped an arm around me. "Come on, sis. How about we make root beer floats when we get home? They always do the trick."

Ten root beer floats wouldn't take away the sorrow and pain I was feeling.

Chapter 21

Maiken

K ade waltzed in with damp hair, a crisp buttoned-up shirt, jeans, and crinkles around his eyes. I swore he'd aged ten years since my brothers and sister started school only several weeks ago.

He crossed the room. "Good morning." He sat in the chair beside my bed. "For someone who was hit by a car, you look pretty darn good."

I would laugh if it weren't for the pain. "How are Emma, Ethan, and Marcus?"

"You should be asking about your mom," he said.

My pulse spiked. I had thought of my mom, but I didn't need to ask about her. I knew she would be beside herself with worry.

He folded one leg so that his ankle rested on the top of his other leg. "I assured her you were fine."

"Did you finally tell her everything?" I imagined he did only because of the accident, which was probably the final straw for Kade to kick us out and send us to Georgia.

"Right now, all she knows is that you got hit by a car. But all of you will have a chance to tell her about your behavior. She's flying in next week. She would get here sooner, but she sold your aunt Denise's house and needs to finalize all the paperwork."

That meant nothing was keeping her in Georgia. We could live as a family again.

"Have you seen the doctor yet?" Kade asked.

"I think he's scheduled to come in shortly." The nurse on shift that morning had told me Dr. Navar would go over the test results with me. But whatever the CT scan and MRI revealed, I still couldn't move my feet or legs. "Kade, I'm really scared."

He leaned forward. "Dude, I know you are. Listen, you're a fighter. So whatever the news, you need to stay positive."

"He's right," Dr. Navar said, walking in.

I shifted my attention to the tall dark-haired doctor, and my heart raced for the finish line. I couldn't tell whether he had good news or not, but the fact that he was standing in my room was enough to get the adrenaline going.

He settled at the foot of my bed. "Test results show a mild concussion. No broken bones and no fractures. You do have swelling around your lower lumbar region, and the MRI shows a herniated disk."

"Is that why I can't move my legs?" I crossed my fingers.

"More than likely. The slipped disk is cutting off nerve impulses. Adding to that is the swelling."

"So I'll walk again. Right?" *Say yes.*

I couldn't go through the rest of my life not playing basketball, or walking down the aisle whenever I got married, or even having sex. It would suck if I couldn't even experience that for the first time.

"There is the possibility of nerve damage, but I suspect you will." He proceeded to run the same tests on my feet as he had the day before. "Tell me if you feel anything."

I clenched my jaw, concentrating. "Nothing."

Kade shoved his hands through his hair, hard. "What are the options to repair the disk?"

Dr. Navar went over to a small computer and typed in some notes. "Physical therapy, which I would recommend first, and as a last resort, surgery. Maiken, any more dizziness or nausea this morning?"

"No, sir. My head is sore, though."

"We'll keep you one more day for observation, and then you can go home. I want you to rest. I'll send you home with meds to take care of the pain and swelling." He tapped on the keys as he talked. "I want to see you back here in a week. Any questions?" He regarded Kade and me.

"As far as school…" Kade said.

I hadn't been thinking of school. Frankly, if Dr. Navar said I could go, I would beg Kade to let me stay home, at least until I could walk again. I usually didn't care what people thought of me, but I didn't want to hear the whispers or see the pity on their faces.

"He's beat up and bruised pretty badly. And with that herniated disk, he'll be in and out of pain. Let's keep him home until I see him next week. I'll give you a doctor's note." Dr. Navar headed for the door. "Lots of rest, Maiken."

Once he was gone, I held back tears.

"It's good news," Kade said as if he were trying to convince himself more than me. "You'll walk again."

I lifted my shoulders. He was right. Dr. Navar hadn't said I would never walk again. But I still felt all doom and gloom. I should've never gone to homecoming. "I wouldn't call that good news." Good news would be a firm statement that I would walk out of the hospital.

"Not good news?" Marcus sauntered in like he was a cat burglar. His hair was wet and combed off his head, curling around his ears. His blue eyes were brighter than the night before, and no alcohol wafted in. In fact, the scent of Irish Spring soap floated in the air.

"Weren't you supposed to wait in the cafeteria?" Kade said more than asked. "Only one family member in here at a time."

Marcus rolled his eyes. "When do I ever listen?"

Kade pushed to his feet. "You're right. You remind me so much of Kelton that I want to pull my hair out." His tone was somewhat teasing. "I'm going to get coffee."

Marcus sat in the chair as Kade left. "The doc didn't give you good news? What is it?"

Oh, the fact that I couldn't feel any sensation in my legs, or that I was in pain, or that I might not play basketball or even walk again.

Dr. Navar didn't say you were permanently paralyzed. It's only your disk.

Even if I did walk again, would I be in the same physical shape I'd been in before the accident? Would I be able to do jump shots or go in for a layup?

I inhaled, grateful for the oxygen tube in my nose, which was helping to get air in my lungs without me having to take in deep breaths. "Right now, I can't walk. The doctor says I have a slipped disk in my lower spine."

"Fuck," he rushed out in a tone that was laced with pain and sorrow. "But you'll walk again? This is all my fault." He threw his head in his hands. "I brought Sloane into our lives."

While Sloane was the reason I was in the hospital, and as furious as I was with her for what she'd done, there was fault to go around. I hadn't seen her coming. Marcus didn't have to be such an ass and get drunk. We could talk about what-ifs all night, but we couldn't go back and change what had happened. Not only that, I could tell him until I was blue in the face not to blame himself, but he wouldn't listen.

"This isn't your fault, bro. It was an accident. Besides, I thought you liked her."

"I do, man. She gets me. She's been through hell too."

I wanted to believe that Sloane was good for Marcus, but it was hard when he'd been drinking again while he was with her.

"Why did you drink again?"

He hiked a shoulder. "It helps take away all the bad thoughts I have running through my head." He stared at me pensively as his blue eyes became cloudy. "I miss Dad so fucking much." He covered his face with his hands. "I feel like I want to die sometimes."

I shivered at his last statement. Sure, Dad's death was still hard on me, but I didn't want to die. "I'm worried about you." I remembered something Uncle Martin had told Kade. "What about talking to a shrink? Kody and Lacey have." I was quick to throw the last part in just in case he thought seeing a shrink would be an embarrassment to the family.

"I don't know," he said.

"Would you think about it?"

He nodded. "I'm sorry, too, for being a dick."

I reached out to touch him, but he wasn't close enough. "Look at me." My heart was breaking into a trillion pieces.

Lowering his hands, he blinked away tears.

"I love you, Marcus. We'll get through this. Mom is coming up next week. She sold Aunt Denise's house. So maybe she'll find a house here."

He grinned. It was the first time I'd seen hope in his eyes.

Doctors and nurses hurried by outside the room. The machines around me hummed.

"I'm trying out for the hockey team," he said.

It was my turn to grin. "That's awesome." He reminded me of something. "Do you know their center, Dustin Lane?" Liam had said Dustin wanted to talk to me.

"Yeah, about him—I kind of told him to fuck off when he looked at me funny in the cafeteria the other day. I'll apologize to him."

At the moment, I didn't care about Dustin or what Marcus had done to him. All I cared about was getting better and my family.

"So once the swelling goes down, you'll walk again?" he asked.

"Bro, I will play basketball, have sex, run, and everything else." I had to believe that.

He gave me a cheeky grin. "I didn't even think about sex."

"Well, you shouldn't. You're only fifteen."

He laughed. "Seriously. I'm going through puberty."

I had to laugh with him. I believed we'd turned a huge corner, and no matter what the future held, I had my brother back.

Chapter 22

Quinn

Dazed was the word of the day. I ambled from class to class like a zombie in *The Walking Dead.* Saturday and Sunday came and went, and I hadn't talked to or seen Maiken. I'd planned on visiting him on Saturday at the hospital, but Momma had nixed the idea. She'd spoken to Eleanor Maxwell and found out that only family members were allowed to see Maiken. She'd also learned that Maiken had been discharged on Sunday. After church, I'd been ready to run over to his house until Eleanor again stopped me.

"He's in and out of sleep with the pain meds," she had said.

As desperate as I was to see him, I had to respect my elders. Besides, I wasn't family. I couldn't barge in and demand to see him.

The last few days had been unbearable. I couldn't sleep. I couldn't eat. And I walked around with my head down most of the time. I tried to get the images out of my head of how Maiken's body had landed on top of Sloane's car, rolled off, and splattered on the ground. But it was useless. Anytime I closed my eyes, the images played out like a video stuck on a recurring loop.

The bell rang, signaling the end of Monday… or was it Tuesday? Kids ran out of class, dropping off their assignments to Mr. Brown, my AP US history teacher. He'd given us twenty minutes to summarize the Navigation Act of 1660 and explain how the explosion of trade opportunities prompted the need for better navigational tools.

I sat at my desk, staring at a blank piece of paper. Normally, I would have had the assignment done and turned in within ten minutes, but I hadn't been paying attention. I also hadn't read the required material that past weekend, which was so unlike me. I always completed my homework, did every assignment, passed every quiz and test, and participated in class.

Mr. Brown circled his desk, removing his reading glasses. "Quinn, the bell rang."

I picked up the paper, which only had my name on it, and handed in the blank assignment that I was sure would garner a large red F. "I know."

"This is so unlike you," he said. "What's going on?"

I returned to my desk for my bag. "It's nothing. I'll do better tomorrow." I was entitled to one free pass, at least I thought so.

"Is it about homecoming?" he asked.

I strapped my bag crosswise over my body. "I saw the accident."

He rubbed his gray beard. "How is Maiken?"

Everyone knew about Maiken. He'd been the talk of the entire school that day, as had Sloane and Marcus, especially Sloane. None of the whispers and words about her had been kind. The rumor floating around was that she'd been drunk. I didn't know that for sure, but I knew Marcus had been.

"You have to watch out for her. She was in juvie," I'd heard one girl say at lunch.

Little did they know she'd been in a mental health facility. I could understand her not wanting anyone to know about her personal life. So the question remained—why had she told everyone she'd been in juvie?

"I guess he's okay. His family says he's bruised badly, but no broken bones."

I'd wanted to ask Emma or Ethan or even Marcus more about Maiken, but they hadn't been in school that day either.

I'd called Maiken and even texted him, but he hadn't answered or replied. I knew the pain meds were keeping him sleepy. So I shouldn't be feeling like he didn't want anything to do with me, but I couldn't help it. I was haunted by guilt that hadn't gone away and wouldn't until I saw and talked to Maiken.

"Well, I'll give you one pass on this assignment," Mr. Brown said.

My phone buzzed in my back pocket. I fumbled to retrieve it. *Please let it be Maiken.* But the text was from Liam.

Chase and I are going to work out in the weight room. I'll catch a ride home with him. Stop by the sports complex, and I'll give you my keys.

I replied with a smiley face, even though I was far from planting a smile on mine. Then I headed for the door. "Mr. Brown, I can do the assignment tonight and hand it in tomorrow."

He placed my blank paper on his desk. "No need. Just study for the test tonight. You do remember we have a test tomorrow?"

Vaguely. "Yes, sir."

He returned to his chair while I hurried out.

I wasn't sure why I felt the need to run. But as my legs kicked into gear, I wanted to run far and fast. I jogged down the empty halls of school toward the exit and fresh air. Maybe the cool fall air would wake me up or erase all my self-loathing, despair, and pity.

When I rounded a corner, I felt like I plowed into a wall. Suddenly, I was falling as images of Maiken hitting the ground flashed before me.

"Watch where you're going," a familiar voice barked.

It took me a moment to regain my senses and zero in on Sloane Price.

She was retrieving her bag off the floor while I was picking myself up.

She ran her hands down her black skinny jeans. "Is there a fire? Or are you trying to give me another black eye?" Her tone was condescending.

I fixated on the dark area around her left eye. I could give her one more to make her look like a raccoon. "Why are you so…" I couldn't find the right word, although I envisioned my hands around her neck. Ever since she'd come to Kensington, Maiken had been different—

moody, angry, and preoccupied. I knew he was worried about Marcus, but he'd been especially on edge since Sloane's party.

"Cat got your tongue?" she snipped.

"Aren't you supposed to be in jail?" I knew Officer Daniels hadn't arrested her. I'd overheard the conversation between Daddy and Officer Daniels at church on Sunday. The accident took place in a dimly lit parking lot at night. If it had been a crosswalk, the law was more definitive in favor of the pedestrian. Not only that, Maiken had darted out. So in essence, he could be partly to blame. But really it was my fault, not Maiken's.

Regardless, Sloane had had no alcohol in her system. She hadn't fled the scene, and she'd been cooperative with the police. The only way Sloane could pay for what she'd done was if Maiken and his family pressed charges.

She let out an evil laugh. "Everyone wants to commit me." She rolled her eyes. "You people are all alike. Mind your own business." Grasping the strap of her bag, she marched away.

Maybe the word commit set me off, or maybe it was her statement "you people are all alike." Either way, I stomped up to her and grabbed her arm.

She looked at my hand then up at me with fury swimming in her brown eyes. "Take your hand off me."

"What is y-your deal? You seem obsessed with the Maxwells." She'd been tied to Marcus. She wore a T-shirt with the title of Kody Maxwell's song on it. She lived down the road from the Maxwells. She'd tried to get a job at the club Kade managed. She was in Maiken's physics class, and I was beginning to believe that wasn't a coincidence. Maybe I was the crazy one.

"Are you saying I'm a stalker?" Her fury morphed into something I couldn't put my finger on.

"Are you?"

She closed her hand into a fist, studying me like I was her science project. She mashed her red lips into a thin line and again marched down the hall. She'd gotten maybe five steps before spinning on her heel and stomping back to me. "You aren't any better than me. I could say you're stalking the Maxwells too."

I snorted. "I'm Maiken's girlfriend."

"And I'm Marcus's girlfriend."

I inched closer to her. "Girlfriends don't get boyfriends d-drunk." *Don't stutter, Quinn.*

She stuck out her chest. "Who says I did?"

"You handed out shots at your party."

She narrowed her brown eyes, which stood out like a beacon in the night in contrast to her white-blond hair. "I didn't force anyone to drink."

"What about homecoming? Where did Marcus get the liquor?"

Shaking her head, she laughed. "Why don't you ask him? I had nothing to do with giving him liquor. That's why you're all alike in this school. You're so quick to judge a new person before you even get to know them."

Suddenly, I was beginning to feel like a stupid girl. I knew better than to presume.

"Then why tell everyone you were in juvie when in fact you were in a mental health facility?"

Her skin paled even whiter. "Mind your own business." Her tone was soft that time, and she once again walked away.

"Sloane, were you the one who started that rumor that Tessa was pregnant?" I'd never come out and asked her.

She flipped me off as she disappeared around a corner.

That dazed feeling I'd had all day tripled. I stomped off like I had many times when I hadn't gotten my way as a kid.

It was time to see Maiken. Whether or not he was awake, I had to see with my own eyes that he was okay. Otherwise, I would die inside.

Forty minutes later, I was parked outside Kade and Lacey's home. The two-story stone-facing structure had large exterior windows and an open L-shaped porch that banked around to one side of the house. Inviting rocking chairs dotted the porch.

I slowly got out of Liam's truck, not sure if being there was the right thing to do. I also wasn't sure if I was ready to see Maiken all battered and bruised.

But for some reason, my legs moved even though my brain seemed stuck on fear. I shuddered as I pressed on the doorbell then held my stomach, willing the nerves to go away.

Kade opened the door, appearing like a giant ready to snap at anyone who dared walk in. At least the tension jumping off him told me so.

I swallowed an elephant. "C-can I s-see Maiken?"

He considered me with a deadpan expression before he stepped out and closed the door behind him. "I'm sorry, Quinn. Not today. His mom is with him, and he's in and out of sleep."

Don't cry. Don't cry. "He doesn't want to see me. Does he?"

Kade waved his arm out. "Walk with me."

The fact that he didn't answer my question was enough to make me want to bawl my eyes out. Nevertheless, I walked on shaky legs with him down a stone path that led to one of the two garages on the property, where my truck was parked.

"Maiken has suffered severe trauma to his body." His tone was soft. "Look, I know first hand what you're going through. But he needs all the rest he can get."

I wanted to see him now. "Can you tell him to at least text me?" At least if I heard from Maiken in some way, I might not flip out as badly as I had been.

"I'll relay the message," Kade said.

Reluctantly, I rounded the truck to the driver's side.

"And, Quinn, I'm sorry that I snapped at you in the emergency room the other night."

I'd forgotten about that. "It's fine," I said as I got into the truck. Emotions were high for everyone.

As soon as I drove way, I broke down in tears. I felt like Maiken had just broken up with me.

Chapter 23

Maiken

My eyes opened as though something were poking me to wake up. I pinched my eyebrows together, concentrating on the tingling sensation traveling down my legs along with the pain in my right leg.

"What is it?" Mom asked.

Mom? I blinked several times, orienting my vision, and found Mom holding my hand so tight. Maybe that was the tingling sensation I'd felt.

"Mom." My voice was hoarse.

She popped out of a chair. "Have some water." She grabbed a cup that was on my nightstand and held it for me while I sipped from the straw.

The cool liquid eased the dryness in my throat. "When did you get here?" Kade had said she was coming up, but I thought it would be later in the week.

She placed the cup back on the nightstand. "Only an hour ago." She sighed. Her brown gaze was soft yet sad. "I've never been so worried in all my life."

"I didn't mean to—"

"Shh. Accidents happen." She sat on the edge of my bed. "You need your strength to get better, not worry about me or anything else."

"I think I feel something in my feet."

Her eyebrows shot to her hairline, and she jumped up. All the tension seemed to leave her as she found my right foot and squeezed. "Do you feel that?"

I grinned and cried at the same time. "I can."

She dragged one of her nails over the top of my foot. "That?"

I nodded.

"Wiggle your toes."

So I did. "I have a shooting pain down my right leg."

She tested my left foot. "How about this foot?"

"I can feel more in that foot than my right." Suddenly, I wanted to get up and walk.

As though she knew what I was thinking, she rushed to the side of my bed. "Don't you dare get up." She fluffed my pillow. "Baby steps."

Kade knocked on the open door before he sauntered in. He looked less tired than he had when he'd been in the hospital with me. Although I suspected a huge weight had been lifted now that my mom was there.

He settled at the bottom of my bed. "What's going on?" He looked at Mom then me.

"I have feeling in my feet."

His grinned from ear to ear. "Fantastic."

I smiled so wide too. Maybe things were looking up.

"Who was at the door?" Mom asked.

Kade regarded me. "Quinn was here."

My smile got even bigger if that were possible. "Was?"

Mom patted my arm. "You don't need any visitors right now."

It wasn't as though Quinn would throw herself at me. Or maybe she would. Still, I wanted to see my girl. *Not like this, you don't.* Maybe it *was* best she didn't see me like this. Still, she had to be going nuts. If I were in her shoes, I would break down doors to see her. "Where's my phone?" I had to at least hear her voice.

"You can call her later," Mom said in her motherly tone. "Now that you're awake, I would like to talk to all of you before I have to return to Georgia."

I glanced at Kade to gauge if Mom knew about more than just the accident. But as usual, his blank expression gave me no indication one way or the other. It didn't matter. It was time to come clean. It was time to apologize for not taking better care of my siblings like I'd promised her.

"Did the rest of the family come with you?" I asked.

"No. A dear friend of mine is watching them since they're in school. Which is why I need to get back."

Kade started for the door. "I'll round up the others. They're down in the media room."

Mom used that time to go to the bathroom.

I wiggled my feet, elated that I could at least feel something again.

Voices carried up the stairs as my siblings piled in.

Emma gasped. "You're moving your feet."

Marcus and Ethan ran to my bedside.

"Do it again," Ethan said.

"Can you get up?" Marcus asked.

The door to the Jack-and-Jill bathroom opened. "He's not getting up yet." Mom returned.

The room dropped into a thick silence. I got the feeling they knew we were about to get a talking to, and when Mom was angry, we listened.

"Find a seat," Mom said. "It's time that we have a very serious discussion."

Marcus sat in the dining chair next to my bed, Ethan went over to the window seat, and Emma found a spot at the bottom of my bed.

I wanted to ask them how school was or if they'd seen Quinn, but Emma was in her pajamas, which told me she hadn't gone to school.

Mom's features tightened as she stood near the dresser adjacent to the bathroom door. "Is there anything any of you want to tell me?" She had a way of giving us a chance to come clean before she dove in to yell or reprimand us.

Marcus hung his head. "I'm the one you need to yell at. I was drinking."

My jaw came apart. I honestly didn't think Marcus would fess up to what he'd done. Considering the way he'd been acting the last few months, I had been afraid he would give Mom a hard time.

Mom lost her mean motherly expression. "Young man, as much as my heart breaks over that, your father would be more disappointed in you."

Marcus stayed silent, not meeting her gaze.

"Kade and Lacey have opened their home and arms for all of you, and this is the way you treat them?" Her tone was even. "Starting today, things will be different. The other kids and I will be returning on Christmas break. In the meantime, I will be house hunting with the help of Kade and Aunt Eleanor." She paused, her lips thinning. "I understand that your father's passing has been difficult. But drinking isn't the way to cope. Fighting isn't either. I'm sorry I haven't been there for all of you, but if things don't change, then maybe military school will give you the structure you need."

The air in the room thickened. I was even freaking out inside as knots spun into a web. I was considering the military one day, depending on whether I could get a college or a basketball scholarship. Hell, maybe that wouldn't happen now considering the way my back was all messed up.

Marcus and Ethan tensed. Emma's eyes got super big. I didn't think Mom had included Emma in her threat.

Mom didn't move from her spot as she swung her gaze around the room. "Drinking, rebelling, fighting, and car accidents aren't something that I will stand for. I know growing up is hard. Teenage years are tough. But I am now your mom *and* dad. Help me out."

"Mom." My voice was barely above a whisper. "We just want to be a family again."

I wasn't sure if things would change or if Marcus would continue down the path he was on. Even though my mom was military tough, one parent couldn't handle five teenagers. I included my fourteen-year-old brother, Jasper, in that calculation even though he wasn't there. He might very well follow in Marcus's footsteps. Not to mention, the younger siblings would be teenagers before long.

"I think I want to see a shrink," Marcus blurted out.

Suddenly, I felt as though I'd done my job as a big brother. He'd listened to me. Or maybe he didn't want to end up in a mental health facility like Sloane. Either way, I believed both Sloane and I had affected Marcus in a positive way, although I was sure the accident had scared him straight too.

"Me too," Emma said. "Aunt Eleanor told me Kody went to one in town, and the doctor helped him."

Mom's eyes filled with tears. "I like that idea. I'll talk to Uncle Martin. He'll refer us to one of his colleagues."

Ethan didn't add anything, and neither did I. My priority at the moment was to get back in physical shape. But I wasn't opposed to the idea of seeing a mental health professional since I'd recommended a shrink to Marcus.

"Between now and when I return, Kade and Uncle Martin have my full support on discipline. You will respect them, listen to them, and follow their rules. Understood?"

"Yes, ma'am," the four of us said in unison.

Marcus hopped up and hugged Mom.

Tears cascaded down her cheeks as she rubbed Marcus's back. "We're going to get through this. I promise."

Then Ethan and Emma were hugging on them.

Even though I couldn't jump in, I was dancing inside. Nevertheless, maybe I could move.

Lifting my legs, I groaned. When I did, all eyes rounded to me.

Ethan and Marcus flew to my bedside.

"Don't move," Ethan said.

Then before I knew what was happening, my family was at my side, each of them hugging me as best they could.

Once the tears subsided, Mom said, "One last thing. Maiken is going to need help. I'll talk to the school. I'm sure you can get your assignments online. Ethan and Marcus, both of you need to help him with his daily grooming and bathroom needs before you head to school and when you get home."

Life was already a million times better. I had sensation back in my legs, and my family was on the mend. All I needed now was to get back in tip-top shape so I could play basketball and do all the other things that came with being a teenager and having a girlfriend.

Chapter 24

Quinn

The dewy grass glistened from the morning sun as I made my way into school like a snail. I'd had a sleepless night, holding my phone, hoping Maiken would at least text me.

"Quinn," Celia shouted from somewhere behind me.

I slid out of the way of traffic as kids trampled in through the main doors.

She held on to the straps of her backpack. "Why aren't you answering my texts?"

Oh, because I'm depressed and don't feel like talking. Because Maiken doesn't want to see me. Because I caused him to get hit by a car.

Tears stung my eyes.

She pursed her pink-stained lips. "Oh, you still haven't seen Maiken?"

I shook my head. "His family won't let me."

She rubbed my arm. "Give him time."

I wasn't naive to the fact that he was resting and hurting, but a simple text from him would calm my racing heart, not to mention the guilt and bad thoughts I couldn't shake.

"Ever since school started, I feel like we've grown apart," I confessed to Celia.

"I don't understand," she said. "You two are the *it* couple. He loves you, and you love him."

Doubt, strong and powerful, sat heavy in my stomach. I'd given him my heart, but he might just hand it back to me.

"He's been so focused on Marcus. It's killing me that he won't even text me."

"I know whatever I say isn't going to take away all those crazy thoughts in your head. I'm here for you."

I wasn't just having crazy thoughts but images of the accident.

I cleared my throat to hold in my tears. I felt like I had some sort of ailment where I couldn't stop crying. "I want to hear his voice." I wanted Maiken to tell me he was okay, and I wanted him to tell me we were still boyfriend and girlfriend.

The first bell rang.

I had the urge to ditch school and ride Apple or hide in the loft in the barn. I couldn't sit through lectures, quizzes, and tests. *Argh!* I had a test in US history—one I'd barely studied for.

A cool breeze ruffled Celia's mane. "Let's go in. Maybe you can tell the nurse you're not feeling well and get a note to go home."

Momma wouldn't buy that excuse. When I'd gotten home from Kade's house, I'd cried in Momma's arms. She'd pretty much said the same thing Celia had just said. Still, neither advice was helping take away the dread I was feeling.

Nevertheless, I walked into school, listening to Celia talk about Liam and how she was so excited to be dating my brother. I was happy for her, but I tuned her out. I knew I was being a terrible friend, but my world was crumbling.

Celia nudged me with her elbow. "Look."

The jolt of her gesture shook me out of my misery. I spied Tessa wagging her red-painted nail at Sloane.

Part of me almost laughed at the sight, only because I remembered those days when Tessa was taunting me. Yet unlike me, Sloane looked bored out of her mind as she picked at a nail. I questioned why she was even putting up with Tessa.

"Quinn, get over here," Tessa ordered in her haughty tone.

Ignoring her, I kept going. If she thought I could be commanded like a dog in training, she had another think coming. Plus, I wanted nothing to do with whatever Tessa was brewing up with Sloane. The two together were triple the trouble.

Tessa raised her voice. "Quinn!"

The din of kids talking in the hall quieted.

"You should see what she wants," Celia said as we continued to our lockers.

"Not interested." I wanted to wallow in my own misery, not hear anyone else's.

Again, Tessa called my name in an even louder voice.

I spun on my heel and stomped over to them for nothing more than to quiet Tessa. With the mood I was in, I would probably punch Tessa like I had Sloane.

"What!" I regarded Tessa and then Sloane. "Whatever it is between you two, I want nothing to do with it."

"You'll want to hear this," Tessa said in a calmer voice. "I found out who wrote that rumor about me on the mirror in the girls' restroom."

Now she had my attention. Not that I would do anything about it, but I would like to know. Ninety percent of me knew Sloane was the one, but the bigger question was why?

"Do you have proof?" Sloane asked in an arrogant tone.

Tessa's dark eyes burned brightly as she dug into her bag and whipped out a leather journal.

Sloane snapped to attention, snagging it from Tessa. "Where did you get that?"

"Shall I recite a quote from your journal?" Tessa asked.

Sloane's face turned almost as white as her hair—a sharp change from the cocksure attitude she'd worn a minute ago.

I tensed, feeling empathy for Sloane. I knew all too well the horror she was going through being bullied by Tessa. The fact that Sloane was the perpetrator paled in comparison to having all her personal thoughts in the hands of the one girl who could destroy a person, and for that, my empathy and sympathy went up a thousand notches.

Celia, who I didn't realize had followed me, gasped.

Regardless, I had to ask, "Why?" Sloane didn't know Tessa or me.

"According to a journal entry," Tessa said, "she doesn't like you or me. And Marcus Maxwell told her that we were enemies. But why say I was pregnant?"

Sloane rolled her eyes. "I'm creative. Think about it. Rich girl. Popular girl. You care what people think. And the worst rumor is you're pregnant."

I didn't agree that was the worst rumor, but considering Tessa, then maybe so. However, the bigger question was why Sloane had lied about being in juvie. I had a feeling she didn't want anyone to know where she'd really been. Then again, maybe she had been in both. But I couldn't ask her that without divulging the truth. I might not care for Sloane, but I wouldn't want people to know if I had been in a mental health facility.

"I've never done anything to you," Tessa fired back.

"You looked at me the wrong way that day you saw me in the admin office. Then when you were talking to me in the library one day, your attitude said you were better than me." She pushed out her shoulders. "I'm sure you don't like many people for the way they look or act."

I wouldn't argue with Sloane on that one. And I was sure the reason she didn't like Tessa was the same reason she didn't like me. I hadn't treated her with fairness, respect, or kindness.

Tessa scrunched up her nose, not saying a word.

Sloane got in Tessa's face. "You can spread all the rumors you want about what I have in my journal. There's nothing in it that will make me crumble. In fact, if you have read it, then you know I have mostly poems and songs that I've written. I also talk about how school sucks and a lot about how you're a bitch." Sloane pushed my shoulder as she stalked off.

"Sloane," Tessa said. "I wouldn't leave your secrets lying around a girls' restroom."

Like Sloane had done to me the day before, she stuck out her middle finger as she bobbed through the crowd.

"Can you believe that?" Tessa huffed.

I could believe just about anything.

I watched Sloane as she met Marcus, who was sauntering toward her as though he could command a crowd. His tall stature, his blue eyes, and the way he swaggered all reminded me so much of Maiken, except for one difference. Maiken exuded compassion. Marcus gave me the impression the world was out to get him.

The two hugged before Sloane said something to him. He glanced past her and glared our way.

Whatever. I stomped to my locker, still moody and irritated.

Celia followed. "I really don't like Sloane."

"She has problems like all of us." That was all I could add without divulging Sloane's secret.

I opened my locker, when Marcus and Sloane strolled by. The two were disgustingly sweet to one another, and their gooeyness for each other only made me want to cry as I thought of Maiken.

"Marcus, how's Maiken?" I asked.

He hardened his jaw. "Leave my brother alone. You've done enough to tear our family apart."

My head went back while my eyes bugged out of my head. "So y-you're b-blaming me for his a-accident? I wasn't the stupid person w-who hit h-him." I snarled at Sloane.

"But you did distract him. If you hadn't, he would be walking," he said in a tone that was dripping with poison. "So it's your fault."

Maiken isn't walking? Does that mean he's paralyzed? But I couldn't bring myself to ask him the latter. I would die, simply and utterly die if he couldn't walk, couldn't play the one sport he loved more than life itself.

"Marcus," Sloane said softly. "That wasn't nice."

I let out a laugh, although it was a cauldron of nerves, evil, shock, guilt, and horror. Sloane Price had some compassion inside her. Regardless, if Marcus wanted to throw stones, I was in the mood too.

I pulled out all the hatred I could and glued it to my glare then stepped up to Marcus. "It seems to me that if you hadn't been acting like such a p-poor me and doing stupid s-shit like drinking, then maybe your brother would be in school and walking." *And holding me. And kissing me.* "Looks to me like it's all your f-fault."

He rolled his eyes, grabbed Sloane's hand, and the two disappeared amid the students gawking as though they were watching an A-list movie.

Yeah, he'd hit a nerve. I might have been blaming myself, stewing on what-ifs and wishing I could go back and change what had happened. But I didn't need him to tell me I was at fault when he'd played a role in Maiken's accident.

The final bell rang.

I couldn't go to class. I couldn't even see straight. Returning to my locker, I slammed the door, gripped the straps of my bag, and headed for the exit.

Celia caught up to me. "Where are you going?"

"I'm skipping school."

She sucked in air. "For real? You and I have never ditched school."

"I am. Not you. You don't need to get in trouble because of me."

"You're not forcing me," she said.

The moment the fall air hit me was the moment all my pent-up emotions came barreling out, and I screamed.

Celia froze. "Should I call the nurse or maybe a shrink?"

I giggled, and the act was freeing until I thought of Maiken not walking. Then I was crying.

I started in the direction of downtown. I had no idea what I was doing or where I was going. Liam had the keys to his truck.

She clutched my arm. "You're kind of scaring me. I've never seen you like this."

I'd never seen myself like this. I'd always been reserved, quiet, kept to myself, and never told anyone off. If I were being honest, I'd kind of enjoyed smarting off to Marcus. Maybe Tessa had taught me a thing or two when she'd bullied me. Because I wasn't letting anyone walk all over me.

Silence surrounded us as we ambled down the sidewalk along the parking lot, heading away from school. When we reached the very edge of where the sidewalk ended, my phone buzzed in the back pocket of my jeans.

With shaky fingers, I managed to snag it without dropping the expensive piece of technology.

Celia looked at my phone with me. "Oh my. See? All your worries should go away now."

I shuddered as I read the text from Maiken. *I'm in and out of sleep with pain meds. Just thinking about you.*

I cried for the millionth time in the four days since his accident.

I responded immediately. *I miss you.*

Then I added a heart emoji.

I thought about asking him if he could walk or ask the several other questions I had, but I would rather ask him in person.

Quinn: *Can I see you?*

Maiken: *My mom is here, and I'm not allowed visitors right now. I'll let you know when. Love you, babe.*

I brought my hand to my mouth as my tears flowed freely. I wasn't crying because he couldn't see me, but because he loved me, and that was all I needed for now.

Chapter 25

Maiken

Ten days had passed since the accident, and in that time, I'd regained all the feelings in the lower half of my body. Walking was a challenge, or more accurately, shuffling across the room and into the bathroom made me feel like I was in my nineties.

Mom had returned to Georgia. My brothers and Emma were in school all day, which left me to sit and watch TV in one of the comfy chairs Kade had brought up to my room or text Quinn, whom I hadn't seen since homecoming. Mom and Kade had been adamant about visitors. But in all honesty, I didn't argue. The pain meds kept me groggy. I felt like crap, and I really didn't want Quinn or even the guys from the basketball team to see me. I'd barely taken a shower. So that was another reason.

I did want to look my best for Quinn. I couldn't have borne to see the look on her face if she'd seen me the way I had been in the hospital or even in the days following.

"Ethan." I raised my voice. "Are you coming in or not? I want to take a shower before Quinn gets here." Sadly, I needed help to get into the bathroom in the event that my legs gave out.

Regardless, it was a big day for me. I'd been dying to see my girl. But I looked like I'd stuck my head in a wind tunnel that had grease in the air, and I smelled like I'd slept in a dumpster all night.

Ethan ambled in, dressed in sweats and a baggy T-shirt. He'd just gotten home from football practice. I would've asked Marcus, but he wasn't home, and of course, I couldn't ask Emma, although she would've helped me if she had to.

Ethan came over to the chair. "Let's see if you can walk by yourself. Didn't Dr. Navar say to try to move as much as you can now on your own?"

I bit my lip. "Yeah, but easier said than done." I'd had my appointment with Dr. Navar the day before.

"I'm glad to see that you're on the mend faster than I expected," he'd said.

And now that I was, he'd recommended physical therapy. But even before I'd seen him, Uncle Martin had set up an appointment with a local chiropractor he knew that specialized in herniated disks. I was scheduled to see the chiropractor the next day. I was excited at the possibility that a decompression machine might help my bulging disk heal faster than physical therapy.

Ethan stayed at my side as I shuffled into the bathroom on my own. If I didn't jerk or move a certain way, I had minimal pain.

Once I was in the shower, Ethan said, "Call me if you need help. I'll be right in my bedroom."

I was going to try to take care of my hygiene all on my own. I soaped up and showered as quickly as I could. The longer I stood, the more pain resonated in my back. Twenty minutes later, I was clean, smelling better, and dressed.

I slowly eased myself back into the comfy chair.

Ethan sat in the window seat, watching me, ready to help. "I'm proud of you, dude. You're getting so much better."

I chuckled. "Not fast enough. I keep thinking of basketball and if I'll be able to play."

He leaned forward, bracing his elbows on his knees. "The way you're going, sure."

One beat ticked by.

"Bro, can I ask you something?" Ethan sounded like he was about to deliver bad news.

I adjusted a pillow behind me. "I'm listening."

"Do you think Mom would send us to a military school?"

I hadn't had a second thought of military school. I also hadn't thought of much during the last week. I'd spent time with Mom for the three days she was there. We'd surfed the net, looking for homes in the area with at least six bedrooms. She'd found a farmhouse not far from the Maxwell property that was for sale. I'd told her that I could check it out with Kade now that I was slowly getting on my feet.

"Has that been bothering you?"

Aside from my own problems, house hunting for Mom, and doing my school assignments, I hadn't talked to Ethan, like seriously talked to him, about school and life in general. That was something we'd done many times when we'd shared a bedroom.

"Or are you asking because Marcus has done something stupid?" That thought rolled into my mind faster than I could blink.

Marcus had been more relaxed as of late, but it wasn't far-fetched to think he could relapse. I knew he wanted to see a shrink, but the last I'd heard, Uncle Martin was working on setting up an appointment.

"He's fine. But I get this sinking feeling that Mom won't be able to handle all eight of us."

"That's why we need to be the adults. We need to continue to help her. We need to be there for Marcus and the rest. Jasper will be in high school next year. So he'll need help too." Freshman year in high school had sucked for me. I'd felt alone and lost. Then again, I was the first of my siblings in high school. "We just need to have each other's backs."

Ethan rose. "Anyway, I've been thinking a lot about military school. I don't want to leave you guys, but maybe it would be good for me."

I could feel creases forming on my forehead. "Why do you sound like you don't want to go, though? Are you afraid I would get mad?"

He shrugged. "I don't want to leave you to take on more responsibility."

"Dude, I don't want you to go, but if military school is what you want, then go for it." I would hate to see him go. But maybe he needed something like military school, much like Marcus and Emma wanted to see a shrink.

He dragged a hand through his brown hair. "I don't know. But I'm glad I have your support."

Kade's voice filtered in. "He's in his room."

Quinn? I didn't hear the doorbell.

Ethan squeezed my shoulder. "Have fun. You know, once you get back to yourself again, maybe you should consider losing your virginity. Maybe all of us boys should." He laughed as he padded into the bathroom and closed the door.

Quinn giggled at something Kade had said. Then my face heated. Maybe she'd heard Ethan.

Nah. He'd spoken in a low voice.

Regardless, my cheeks felt like an inferno as my pulse held steady, waiting for her to walk into the room.

Chapter 26

Quinn

K ade gestured to the door on the right at the end of the hall. Then he backtracked his steps.

Before I took a step, a door next to me opened, and Marcus walked out. We stared at one another like two enemies ready to throw down. I hadn't thought much about our little riff in the hall at school the other day. But I did want him and me to get along, and I didn't hate him.

He ran a hand through his unruly hair, glancing down the hall toward Maiken's room. "Look, I'm sorry I snapped at you. I don't blame you for what happened to Maiken."

Relief coursed through me, but I still wondered if Maiken would blame me.

I shook my head. "No need. Maiken's accident has been difficult for all of us. I'm sorry too."

He shoved his hands in his jeans pockets. "Don't get him too worked up." He gave me a sly boyish grin. "If you get my drift."

My face flushed. "I'll be gentle."

"I've got to run," he said, starting for the stairs.

When he was no longer in sight, I shuddered, smoothed a hand over my hair, pinched my cheeks, and took in a quiet breath to calm the nervous nellies in my tummy, which weren't as bad as they'd been in the emergency room. That night, my entire body had felt like an out-of-control summer storm. Now my apprehension stemmed more from my guilt.

I took one step then another until I was peeking into Maiken's room. When I did, our gazes tangled, and Maiken grinned as though he'd found his lost puppy.

I could be his puppy. I could roll over, and he could pet my belly.

Whether it was his grin or the gleam in his blue eyes that I'd missed so much, my legs were moving, and my feet were sinking into the plush carpet of his bedroom as I ran to him as fast as I could.

I'd never been in Maiken's bedroom, and for some reason, I felt like I was doing something I wasn't supposed to be doing as I quickly took in the bed, desk, TV, dresser, and window seat. The decor wasn't an eye opener except for how big the room was compared with the ones at my house. I had walked into a mansion that was built as though Kade and Lacey had big family plans for lots of kids.

Maiken was sitting in a brown recliner that was situated near the window seat. So I crossed the room, envious of the view he had— colorful fall leaves of orange and reds swayed from the trees, and like my farm, I could see far and wide.

He held out his hand just as I passed him. "Hey."

I didn't know if I should touch him or hug him or even kiss him. Seeing him in the chair with his hair damp and smelling like the woods outside his window, I itched to throw my arms around him. But I didn't want to hurt him. He'd said his neck and back were sore and in pain. However, his lower back was worse than his neck.

"I'm not going to break," he drawled in a lazy Southern accent.

I giggled. "Did you fly south for ten days and pick up even more of a Southern accent?"

He chuckled. "Do you like it?"

Oh boy! I had goose bumps all over me.

"Can you bring my desk chair over here?" he asked. "I want you close to me."

I could sit on you. I promised Marcus I would be gentle, though.

I did as he asked, setting the chair in front of him before I sat down.

His dreamy blue gaze roamed wild and free all over me.

I could feel my lips spreading into a slow smile. All those nerves inside me vanished little by little.

We examined each other, his chest rising and falling with mine.

"Some girl with butterscotch hair, a smile that makes my heart sputter, and eyes only for me once told me that when we look into each other's eyes for three minutes, our heart rates sync or beat together. So is yours beating as fast as mine?"

I worried my bottom lip, briefly shying away. "Faster than the speed of light?"

He nodded with that smirk that was somehow like a magnet pulling me to him. So I pitched forward, pressing my hands on the arms of his chair, leaned in, and kissed him on the lips. His hands shaped my waist as he stuck his tongue in my mouth.

I moaned, thankful the accident hadn't ruined the way he kissed, soft and tender as our tongues danced to music we'd made together. I got lost in him, in time, in us. I didn't notice that his hands were in my hair, pulling me to him as though he couldn't get enough. I knew I needed more, but the more we kissed, the more heated we would get, and he needed to rest. My arms were shaking to the point that I thought I would collapse on him, which normally wouldn't have mattered if he weren't in pain.

So I pulled away slightly, my forehead resting against his for a brief moment before I returned to my seat.

He studied me. "I've missed you so darn much." His voice was husky and smooth.

His words made me shiver in delight as I rested my hands lightly on his thighs. Thus far, I didn't get the feeling he blamed me. Yet my conscience was evil and prodding me to clear the air.

I had to get all that bottled-up guilt out of me. I could've asked him many times over the last few days when we'd swapped texts, but I believed apologies should be done in person. That way, a person could see someone's body language and the true emotions on his face.

I rubbed his thighs, mostly out of nerves. "I'm really, really sorry. I feel responsible for your accident." I'd cried out all my tears, but little did I know I had one or two more to shed.

He wrinkled his nose. "Babe, it's not your fault. Don't think that for a second." He covered my hands with his. "I think we all blame ourselves. That night was a perfect storm of events that we can't go back and change. I'm on the mend, and I love you. That's all that matters."

I bent over and rested my head on his legs. "I've been a mess. When Marcus said you couldn't walk, I thought I was going to die."

His fingers dove into my hair once again, massaging and rubbing. "There was a moment when I thought I would be in a wheelchair for the rest of my life."

That last line made my muscles tense. I couldn't imagine that, but if he had been paralyzed, it wouldn't have mattered to me. He was still my knight in shining armor, the boy I loved, the boy I wanted to experience everything possible with—the good, the bad, and the ugly.

"No matter what would've happened, I will always be here for you."

He stopped rubbing my head.

I lifted up.

His blue eyes sparkled. "Even if I couldn't walk or do anything like dance with you?"

Dancing wasn't my thing to begin with. Sure, it felt nice to be in his arms, swaying to a slow melody, but life wasn't about a dance or homecoming.

My chin quivered. "Yeah." There was no hesitation on my part. "And if you had to use a wheelchair, then I would sit in your lap while you twirled me around on the dance floor."

Several different emotions flickered across his handsome face—happiness, desire, awe, and love. "I wish I could stand up and twirl you around in my arms right now."

I placed my hand on his heart, desperate to feel if his was beating as fast as mine. Boy, was it ever. "You will soon enough."

His long fingers circled my wrist. "My heart is yours, Quinn Thompson."

I grabbed his free hand and positioned it over my heart. "And mine is yours, Maiken Maxwell."

We sealed our commitment with a long, steamy kiss until I felt his face muscles tighten.

"What is it?" I asked.

He blew out a breath. "A twinge of pain. That's all. It's probably time for a pain med."

"Do you need me to get it?" I would wait on him hand and foot if I had to.

"I'm okay."

I sat back down, apprehensive until he grinned. "I think kissing you is making me dizzy."

I giggled. We probably needed to tamp down the make-out session. So I changed topics. "I punched Sloane and gave her a black eye."

A rumble of laughter barreled out of his chest along with a flinch. "It hurts to laugh. Why?"

I checked my knuckles that had been slightly bruised. "She hit you. And not that this has anything to do with homecoming, but she confessed to spreading that rumor about Tessa being pregnant." I went on to explain what had gone down in the hallway at school.

"I hate that I missed that," he said. "Tessa had to be furious. But speaking of Sloane, Marcus confirmed she's been in a mental health facility. Her father died in a fire."

"What?" I said, expelling shock. "I wonder if he died in a barn fire." Sloane had been crying that day on the farm as she'd stood staring at the barn as though she were afraid to go in.

Maiken was squirming as though he were in pain. "He didn't say, and I didn't ask. Are you and Marcus okay? I heard part of your conversation."

"We're good. Nothing to worry about." I didn't want to burden him with more drama.

He moved in his seat, wincing.

I stood. I probably should let him rest even though I didn't want to go. "I'll get Kade."

"Wait. Talk to me some more."

"You're hurting."

He jutted out his chin. "The doc wants me to move. I've been sitting too long. Help me up."

"Um… are you sure?"

"Stand close in case I fall. I'll do the rest."

I moved the desk chair out of the way quickly then planted myself in front of him. If he fell, he would fall on top of me, which was fine with me since I would cushion his fall.

He rose, slowly and tentatively. When he was on two feet, his jaw tensed in concentration before he took one step then another. He inhaled deeply, and in an instant, he had his arms around me. "Now I'm good. Do you want to dance?"

I giggled, melting into him. "Let's not and say we did. Besides, I've come to the conclusion that parties and dances are bad luck for me."

We had junior prom coming up and senior prom next year, but I wasn't sure I wanted to go now. After all, I'd attended Tessa's holiday gala last Christmas and had fallen into a freezing pool of water. Then I'd been excited to attend Sloane's party—my first true teen party—and Marcus had gotten drunk, causing Maiken to leave as soon as he'd gotten there. Then there was homecoming, which was by far the worst.

His lips brushed my ear. "The next party I go to will consist of me and you and no one else."

"I like that kind of party." I had the perfect venue just for us.

He continued to rub my back. "I like this, us, here, quiet."

I closed my eyes, feeling relaxed for the first time in like forever, feeling him breathe, absorbing him.

"I'm going to be okay, Quinn," he whispered.

I got the feeling he was trying to convince himself.

I held on to him tightly in case he fell. "You know, they say that things happen in threes. Maybe this is the third thing to happen in your life, and from here, it's all sunshine and roses."

He snorted. "I'll take sunshine and roses."

We stayed plastered to each other for a long minute, listening to each other's breathing.

Then I eased away. I wanted him to sit or even lie on the bed, anything to take away his pain. But when I looked up at him, my heart sputtered.

Tears cascaded down his cheeks. "I love you hard, Quinn Thompson."

His words were music to my ears. In that moment in his room, our relationship grew by leaps and bounds, and I knew without a doubt we could conquer anything.

Chapter 27

Maiken

I dusted the snow off the basketball and stomped my feet just inside the sports complex before shaking the white flakes out of my hair.

I couldn't believe it was snowing already, although Halloween had come and gone, and Thanksgiving was right around the corner. I'd been out of school for more than four weeks. I'd missed tons of basketball practices but had kept up with my schoolwork.

Nevertheless, I'd been living in either the chiropractor's office or physical therapy when I wasn't doing assignments and homework. I'd spent time reconnecting with Marcus, Ethan, and Emma. Kade and Lacey had been amazing in helping me get around the house and to appointments. And Quinn had stopped by any chance she had. Her days were filled with homework and chores around her farm. Her dad hadn't found anyone to help out yet.

I'd thought about giving him a hand, but I was saving all my energy for basketball. I'd suggested to Ethan and Marcus that they should apply for a job at the farm, especially with Christmas coming soon. Mr. Thompson would be hiring for his Christmas tree business. Ethan was thinking about it, but Marcus was busy with learning how to ice-skate. He didn't make the hockey team because his skating skills sucked.

My life was getting better, particularly now that Mom and the rest of the family were moving back to Ashford. She'd purchased a farm-house in between the Maxwell estate and Quinn's farm.

So the one thing missing was basketball. I was praying I could move up and down the court without any pain or discomfort. Dr. Navar had said to take it slow and not to expect too much in the beginning.

The gym was empty when I walked in. I wasn't surprised. With the snow falling hard outside, kids had scattered quickly after school. Coach had even canceled practice. But I couldn't wait to shoot a few rounds.

After I shucked my coat, I bounced the ball over to the top of the key then stared at the net. Equal parts of euphoria and dread washed over me. Thoughts ran rampant and had been since that awful night. Could I still shoot, jump, and move my body like I had before the accident?

I was deep in my head and didn't hear anyone come into the gym until Chase Stevens's voice penetrated my ears.

"Well, are you going to shoot or stand there like a moron?" Chase taunted.

I blinked once then twice and found him standing under the net with a smirk on his pimpled face.

I threw him the finger. "Nice to see you too."

He tucked his hands into his coat pockets. "First day back. How was it?"

Sucked. I shrugged. "Fine, I guess." Sitting all day in a hard chair had been a challenge on my lower back.

"Well, the team needs you. Do you think you'll be one hundred percent by the first game next month?"

Man, I prayed I was. "For sure." I would do anything, no matter the pain, to be ready to play.

"This is my final season before I graduate. So we need to win games." He wrinkled his dark brows. "Scouts will be watching."

"I know, dude. We'll win games." But winning games wasn't what scouts looked for. They looked at shooting percentages, rebounds, teamwork, and all the other skills that made up a great basketball player. "So you think you'll get into Villanova?" He and Liam were seniors, and both were waiting to hear if they had been accepted into their colleges of choice.

"I sure hope so," he said. "So let's see what you got."

Standing at the top of the key, I bounced the ball a few times as my heart raced. I'd been playing since I was a little boy. I shouldn't be so nervous.

Get out of your head and shoot the damn ball.

Taking a breath, I shot the ball. It hit off the rim and bounced toward the bleachers.

Chase darted out, grabbed it, and threw the ball to me. "Try again." His tone made him sound like the coach.

I kept shooting and missing. The good news was I didn't feel any pain in my lower back. But I was afraid to jerk right or left or step the wrong way, which was probably holding me back.

Maybe playing wasn't going to happen this season. *You've only had the ball in your hands for minutes. Give yourself a chance.*

The door to the gym creaked open, and Sloane Price sashayed in. Her white-blond hair had grown over her ears, and she was dressed in jeans, boots, and a flannel shirt.

"What does she want?" Chase mumbled, sounding as though he didn't want her anywhere near me.

I hadn't seen Sloane since homecoming and for a very good reason. Marcus had tried to get me to talk to her, and I'd refused. I hadn't been ready to see her or listen to her. The cops had asked if I wanted to press charges, but I didn't. I'd been as much at fault as her that night. Still, I'd expected to see her in physics that morning, but she hadn't been in class.

"Maiken," Sloane said. "Can we talk?"

Now was as good a time as any to clear the air, although I really wanted to concentrate on basketball.

"Dude, I'll catch you later." Chase gave me a manly hug. "Oh, the team is going over to Shakers tonight if you want to join us. Bring Quinn."

Getting out of the house and hanging with the team and Quinn was just what the doctor ordered. "I'll see you tonight."

Once Sloane and I had the gym to ourselves, she sat down on the first row of the bleachers. "I'm so sorry, Maiken. I've been wanting to tell you that, but I've been afraid."

With the ball in my hand, I sat down next to her. I didn't have as much hatred toward her as I thought I would, maybe because she wasn't sporting her cocky attitude and seemed truly sorry. "Why were you afraid?"

"I hit my boyfriend's brother. I was an idiot, embarrassed, and all I kept thinking was I screwed up again."

"Screwed up again?"

She cast her gaze at her hands, which she was wringing in her lap. "I was responsible for my dad's death."

My jaw hit the floor.

"That night was one of the coldest on record." Her voice was barely a whisper. "All I wanted to do was keep the horses warm. We didn't have any fancy equipment. So like every extremely cold night, I set up a space heater—anything to make sure the horses were okay. I thought I closed the barn door before I went up to the house, but I didn't close it tight enough. The wind was high that night and blew open the doors. When we realized what was happening, I didn't even think. I ran into the barn to save the horses. My dad ran in to save me, but he never made it out."

"How did you?"

"A firefighter found me before the roof collapsed."

I had no words.

She flicked tears off her cheeks with the sleeve of her flannel shirt. "So I'm really sorry. I'm always doing stupid shit."

I draped my arm around her, which was the only way I knew how to tell her I accepted her apology. A large part of me hurt for her. I knew all too well what it felt like to lose my dad.

"She told you," Marcus said.

I jerked my head up. I hadn't even heard Marcus come in. But I wasn't looking at my brother. I was looking at my beautiful Quinn, who had as much sadness swimming in her eyes as I felt in my chest.

Marcus helped Sloane to her feet and held her in his arms. I always thought Marcus had a big heart, but given his actions over the past few months, I'd started to wonder if that were true. Not anymore. My brother was her rock.

Quinn sat down next to me. "Are you okay?"

A tear dropped on my leg. It took me a second to realize I was crying. "I'm good."

Marcus mouthed "thank you" to me.

I hadn't done anything. "Sloane, thank you for telling me."

She turned in Marcus's arms so her back was against his front. Her eyes were covered in mascara.

"We're good," I said. "But do me one favor. Take care of my brother." I was hoping she got the unspoken message to make sure he doesn't drink. After all, she had two years on him, and she should be more responsible.

She craned her neck up at him, batting her lashes. It was then I saw that she really liked my brother. "I will."

Marcus and Sloane started for the door.

"Hey, Sloane," Quinn said. "Were you ever in juvie?"

I'd completely forgotten that about Sloane, and with all that had been going on, I hadn't even thought to ask Marcus.

Sloane spun on her heel, and a defeated expression crossed her features. "I spent one day in juvie for something that I would rather not talk about. I have enough rumors going around school about me anyway."

Quinn furrowed her brows. "But your mom told my dad you weren't in juvie."

"My mom doesn't share everything with people," Sloane said.

Marcus draped an arm around her. "It isn't anyone's business."

Then they were gone.

He was right. I didn't care anyway. As long as my brother was happy and wasn't doing stupid shit, I was cool with Sloane.

Quinn covered my hand with hers. "I've asked her once before about juvie. I was surprised she came clean."

"Did you know about her dad?"

"Marcus told me the story while we were out in the hall."

"So are you sure you and Marcus are okay?" She'd never told me the details of what had happened between her and my brother except that it was an emotional time and it was over with now.

She nudged her shoulder into mine. "Marcus and I are cool."

We sat there for a long minute, the bright lights flickering. My heart went out to Sloane for her loss, but it was time for me to concentrate on basketball and my girl.

I stood. "Enough about Sloane and Marcus. Shoot with me."

Quinn giggled. "I can't play."

"You know the game." The first time I met her, she'd spouted off stats about the Celtics.

She rolled her eyes. "I'm afraid I might show you up."

I belted out a laugh. "Well, pretty lady, let's see what you got." I handed her the ball.

She bounced the ball over to the net, albeit awkwardly. The she held the ball to her chest and pushed out with her arms. The ball reached the bottom of the net.

I retrieved the ball. "Here. I'll show you." I got behind her and placed the ball in her hands. Leaning over slightly, I blew in her ear. "You can show me up anytime."

She moaned softly.

I began peppering kisses up and down her neck. "You and the ball need to become one."

She snorted. "You're making things up."

Anything to keep kissing her.

Letting go of the ball, she turned and pressed her hands to my chest. "You're supposed to be practicing."

The sound of the ball bouncing away echoed.

I gave her a sly grin. "I am."

She swatted at me. "Not making out, you big hunk. Basketball."

I dragged a finger over her lips. "Are you sure? We could find a dark place behind the bleachers."

She flipped her hair over her shoulder and started to walk away. "I saw Chase, and he said we're going to Shakers. So I'll see you later."

I pouted as I watched her wiggle her hips right out of the gym. It took me a second to shake off all the butterflies Quinn had left behind. Then I dove into shooting and practicing my basketball moves.

Chapter 28

Quinn

Ten weeks had passed since Maiken had returned to school and basketball. In that time, he'd had a tough road getting back in shape after his accident. According to his doctor, he'd done too much, too soon. It also hadn't helped that he'd fallen one too many times during practices and had pushed himself so hard, he could barely move.

I shivered as I watched Maiken run up and down the court. Every move, jerk, shot, and layup he took, I held my breath. He wanted to do well that night against Lancaster Christian. He wanted to prove to himself that he wasn't broken and that he could jump, shoot, and dribble like he had before the accident.

He hadn't played the handful of games in December and had missed all but one game in January. Now with the season winding down in February, he was only playing in his third game.

I bounced my knee, biting my nails.

"He's in good shape," Christine, Maiken's mom, said at my side. "This is the first time I've seen him relaxed in a game since his freshman year."

Maiken had been on fire last season, but his Mom hadn't been here. Regardless, Maiken wasn't wincing or tense or bending over to catch his breath frequently. I knew bones took a long time to heal. I also knew scar tissue could cause problems too. I'd done a ton of research on the spine and disks after Maiken's accident.

Maiken went in for a layup, but the ball didn't go in, and a lanky boy from Lancaster Christian got the rebound. He passed to his teammate, who in turn dribbled the ball downcourt as Kensington got into defense.

The crowd started chanting, "Defense, defense, defense." With two minutes left in the game, we were down by ten points. I didn't think we had a chance to win. With Maiken out most of the season, the team had struggled to win games. In my opinion, they hadn't found their vibe with one of the other team members who had filled in for Maiken.

Coach Dean was shouting and waving his arm at the team. Kade stood next to Coach, watching intently. Rumor around school was that Coach Dean was retiring after this year and Kade would be taking on the position of head coach.

"How's the new house?" I asked Christine.

She kept her eyes on the court. "It's finally becoming a warm and comfortable home. I do have to thank your dad for all his help."

Christine and her family had moved into a spacious farmhouse that was more than enough for a family of nine, particularly the three acres of wide-open space for the kids to play and roam.

I was digging the location since it wasn't that far from where I lived. In fact, Maiken lived closer now than when he'd been at the Maxwell estate.

The Lancaster crowd applauded when their team scored, and Kensington now had the ball. Again, I bit a nail. By the time the game was over—and there was only one minute left on the clock—I swore I wouldn't have any nails left.

Chase passed the ball to Liam, who bounced it once before passing it to Maiken. Maiken darted right then left before spinning around and charging the net. When he did, one of his opponents went up to block the shot and collided with Maiken, who in turn fell backward.

A collective intake of breath zipped around the Kensington side when his body hit the floor. I brought both hands to my mouth as I jumped up. Even Christine and all his siblings were holding their collective breath.

Maiken lay there, not moving.

Coach Dean, Kade, and the rest of the team crowded around Maiken. All eyes, even those of the Lancaster fans, watched and waited as everyone held their breath.

Kade knelt down as Coach Dean motioned with his hands for the guys to give Maiken some space.

"He's good," Christine whispered.

"Come on, Maiken," I said to myself. "Get up."

Hands gripped my shoulders from behind. Then Celia's voice was in my ear. "Breathe."

I'd forgotten she was there.

On her command, I took a small breath, but it did nothing to rid myself of the overwhelming dread going through me.

Kade straightened as Chase and Liam helped Maiken to stand.

Maiken bobbed his head as if to say he was fine.

A collective sigh echoed in the gym along with a round of applause as Maiken walked around a couple of times then resumed playing.

My heart splintered nonetheless. He'd looked so dejected.

"He'll come back in better shape next year," Christine said. "Back injuries can take a long time to heal."

I knew that, and I had no doubt that Maiken was a fighter. I also knew he would do everything he could to impress the college scouts. After all, his senior year would be his defining moment. Not only that, Maiken had a scout from Georgetown that was interested in him, but according to that scout, he needed to see more play time from Maiken. Apparently, the scout had watched tapes of the Kensington team last year when he'd been interested in Liam.

Speaking of Liam, he had learned the week before that he'd gotten a basketball scholarship to NC State. I thought it would be cool if Maiken followed him, which meant he would follow me to NC State as well. That was *if* I got in.

I didn't want to think that far ahead. I also didn't want to think about not seeing Maiken at school and not being able to steal a kiss in between classes. For now, we had the rest of our junior year and all of our senior year to make memories. And I planned on making the best memories possible.

Chapter 29

Maiken

My basketball season sucked, and I was relieved that the misery of not playing and not helping my team to the playoffs, which didn't happen, had ended when the season finished a month ago. I had to do everything I could to get my body in shape for next year. Otherwise, scouts weren't going to look at me. I only had one college interested, but they hadn't reached out since my sophomore year. I really didn't want to go to Georgetown anyway.

The band 5 Seconds of Summer belted out their song "Amnesia," filling up the barn on our property, which Quinn and I had all to ourselves. It was prom night for her and me and no one else. I had been planning this special night since that day when Quinn visited me while I was laid up after the accident. She didn't want to go to junior prom, and neither did I.

Tiny white lights twinkled from the rafters above. I couldn't believe we were living in a farmhouse with land and a barn. My dad would have been in awe if he were there. He'd always wanted lots of land with apple trees and space to ride four-wheelers and do other outdoor activities with the family. Mom had finally gotten his life insurance and her finances worked out, especially since Aunt Denise had left her with a nice sum of money.

I held on to Quinn as we danced to one of her favorite bands. She pressed her cheek against my chest as the song played. We hadn't talked much since she walked in. Between lots of kissing and dancing, I didn't care to talk anyway.

"Do you think anyone is missing us at prom?" she asked in a low voice.

"Not really."

Celia had been bummed that Quinn had decided not to go to junior prom. But other than her, I didn't think anyone would notice.

"Maiken, have you thought about what will happen after high school?" She sounded sad all of a sudden.

The song came to an end.

I pulled away to study her face. "What's wrong?"

Batting her lashes, she shrugged. "I've been thinking of college, and I'm scared that our lives will be different."

Our lives were already different. Since I'd moved there, so much had happened—good, bad, and even ugly. But the best part had been meeting Quinn. I suspected she was thinking of us and what we had in store.

Would I go to a different college than her? Would we grow apart? The answers to those questions were a mystery. But I could only tell her what was in my heart.

"Baby doll." I mashed my forehead to hers. "No doubt life will be different, but in a good way. We will not break up or grow apart." At least that wasn't my plan. I couldn't imagine what I would do if we weren't dating.

She quivered. "I'm afraid that could happen."

I tensed. "Where's this coming from?" I swore if she was breaking up with me or had thoughts of doing that, I might croak right now.

She sashayed over to the stereo, or rather iPad, to put on another song. I had my playlist that I'd prepared for the night with pop artists she liked along with some of my favorite country artists.

Luke Combs's song "Beautiful Crazy" started playing.

I grinned. I often thought of her when I listened to that song.

She turned and leaned against the table, bringing her finger to her mouth.

My grin faded as my heart tried to beat out of my chest. "You're scaring me." I closed the distance between us then guided her chin up until she met my gaze. "Talk to me."

Her bottom lip quivered. "I want us to go to the same college, but I know that might not be possible."

Junior year wasn't over yet. We had about two plus months before school was out for the summer. Still, I hadn't thought much about the future except getting in tip-top shape for next season. I was banking on a scholarship. Otherwise, I might not be going to any college. Mom didn't have that kind of money to send me to an NCAA school. My backup plan was the military, and if that happened, then I definitely wouldn't see Quinn.

I brushed my lips against hers. "We have time to plan out colleges. Why don't we do that together?" I knew her choice was NC State. Mine was either UCLA or Ohio State, but North Carolina had great colleges within a short drive of NC State.

She gnawed on her bottom lip. "Really? You would consider one of the universities in North Carolina?"

I snaked my hand around to the back of her neck then gently pulled her closer to me. "Any college in the state has a great basketball program. More than that, I would follow you anywhere."

She threw her arms around me. "I love you."

The next song on the playlist started.

I swung her around. "Your butterscotch hair shimmers in the light. Your amber eyes sparkle and ignite. Your lips are soft and taste like berry. Nothing about our relationship is temporary." I set her down. "I mean every word of that." I pressed her hand to my chest. "I give you my heart, Quinn Thompson."

She kissed me, wild and crazy.

Whatever senior year had in store for us, I was ready. I planned to make all kinds of good memories with my girl.

DEAR READER

I hope you enjoyed reading the continuation of Maiken and Quinn's story. There will be one more book in their saga. Come join us in Maxwell Mania and stay up-to-date on Maxwell news: Facebook: https://www.facebook.com/groups/maxwellmania/

When you have a moment, I would super appreciate a quick review. It doesn't have to be long, but would love for you to share your excitement about My Heart to Give. You can leave a review on Amazon, Goodreads or Bookbub . Links to these platforms can be found on the next page.

Reading Order for the Maxwell Family Saga Series.

Have you read Kade Maxwell's story? If not, check out the first book in the Maxwell Series (Dare to Kiss) and meet Kade, Kelton,

Kross, and Kody. http://sbalexander.com/book-series/the-maxwell-series/page/2/

DON'T MISS OUT

Stay up-to-date on sales and new releases. I post frequent updates in my reader group on Facebook. You can join here: Maxwell Mania: https://www.facebook.com/groups/maxwellmania/
Follow me on any of the platforms below or signup for my newsletter at http://sbalexander.com/newsletter or visit my website at http://sbalexander.com

- facebook.com/sbalexander.authorpage
- twitter.com/sbalex_author
- instagram.com/sbalexanderauthor
- amazon.com/author/sbalexander
- bookbub.com/authors/s-b-alexander
- goodreads.com/sbalexander

ALSO BY S.B. ALEXANDER

To read samples and find out where to purchase all books visit:
http://sbalexander.com.

The Maxwell Family Saga:

My Heart to Touch - Book 1

My Heart to Hold – Book 2

My Heart to Give – Book 3

My Heart to Keep - Book 4 (releasing late 2019)

The Maxwell Series:

Dare to Kiss - Book 1

Dare to Dream – Book 2

Dare to Love – Book 3

Dare to Dance - Book 4

Dare to Live - Book 5

Dare to Breathe - Book 6

The Maxwell Series Boxed Set – Books 1-3

The Maxwell Series Boxed Set - Books 4-6

Dare to Kiss Coloring Book Companion

The Hart Series:

Hart of Darkness

Hart of Vengeance - Coming Soon

Hart of Redemption - Coming Soon

Stand Alone Books

Breaking Rules

Rescuing Riley

The Vampire SEAL Series:

On the Edge of Humanity – Book 1

On the Edge of Eternity – Book 2

On the Edge of Destiny – Book 3

On the Edge of Misery - Book 4

On the Edge of Infinity - Book 5

The Vampire SEAL Collection - Boxed Set

ACKNOWLEDGMENTS

Writing and publishing a book takes a village. But I couldn't be more thankful to the one person who gives me the inspiration to do what I love—my husband. He's been such a guiding light as he battles one of the worse diseases with no cure. He fills my heart with so much joy. He always has a smile on his face, he's always laughing, and he's always making sure I'm taken care of. He's my angel. I couldn't do this without him.

I'm also grateful to the team behind me who helps me every step of the way from my editor, RedAdept Editing, my beta readers, my ARC team, my cover designer, Hang Le, and everyone in Maxwell Mania. Thank you, thank you, thank you!

A big hug and mad love for Heather Carver for keeping me focused and motivating me everyday to write, and to Kylie Sharp for always being a phone call away. Love you gals.

Finally, to all the readers and bloggers around the world, thank you for taking a chance on me.

www.ingramcontent.com/pod-product-compliance
Lightning Source LLC
Chambersburg PA
CBHW071119100726
47908CB00008B/2422